Books by Steve Brewer

Lonely Street
Baby Face

Published by POCKET BOOKS

BABY FACE

A BUBBA MABRY, P.I., MYSTERY

Steve Brewer

POCKET BOOKS

New York   London   Toronto   Sydney   Tokyo   Singapore

This book is a work of fiction. Names, characters, places and incidents are products of the author's imagination or are used fictitiously. Any resemblance to actual events or locales or persons, living or dead, is entirely coincidental.

An *Original* Publication of POCKET BOOKS

POCKET BOOKS, a division of Simon & Schuster Inc.
1230 Avenue of the Americas, New York, NY 10020

ISBN: 0-671-74735-5

First Pocket Books printing June 1995

10 9 8 7 6 5 4 3 2 1

POCKET and colophon are registered trademarks of Simon & Schuster Inc.

Cover art by Stephen Peringer

Printed in the U.S.A.

*To Frank Zoretich and my wife, Kelly,
my ports in the brainstorm*

BABY FACE

She wore nothing but white cotton panties. She was stretched across the bed on her face, her feet tangled in the sheets, one knee cocked up like she'd been trying to run. Long brown hair spread out behind her, snarled and twisted. Her young breasts pooled against bare mattress. Her skin looked tawny and firm, but a couple of plum-sized purple bruises had surfaced between her shoulder blades.

The back window dangled open on its hinges, rocking in the wind, mocking me. I holstered my revolver and, knees trembling, stepped around the end of the bed for a better look.

Bruises wrapped around her throat like the skins of overripe bananas. Her head was twisted toward one shoulder, and the odd angle of her neck told me there was no need to hurry about an ambulance.

I knew her. Her name was Deena, and she was maybe fifteen years old. She was new on the Cruise, one of those lost children who fall into prostitution early. I'd sometimes seen her on the street, dressed up in a Catholic school uniform with pleated plaid skirt or a

1

thigh-length baby doll dress, all ready for the johns to take her home and play with her.

She hadn't been on the Cruise long enough to get that hard cast to her face, that tight-lipped bitterness that comes from too many disappointments. Her face was as soft and innocent and full-cheeked as a baby's. The sweetest little baby face.

1

It was another windy Thursday in Albuquerque and I was feeling lower than a toad. It was the end of May, long past the usual end to the spring gales, but that hadn't prevented the hair-snatching, eye-watering wind from sandblasting the city all week.

I cowered indoors, draped over my easy chair like I'd fallen there from the sky, clicking through channels with the TV remote, bathing in the flickering glow. The drapes were drawn and the door was locked and the TV volume was up high, but I still could hear the wind's coyote howl through the walls.

Two sharp raps on the door penetrated my blue haze. I switched off the television and dragged myself to the door. I winced before opening it, bracing for a blast of hot wind. But when I flung the door open, a huge bald man filled my doorway so completely that not a molecule of air seeped in around him.

The man had a face like a coral reef, lumpy and craggy and covered with warts and boils and pustules that looked like they could sprout tentacles if some prey happened by. The growths clustered around his bulblike nose, spread down the creases alongside his thick lips, disappeared into the folds of fat under his chin. They covered his ears, which had turned in on themselves in retreat until they were like wads of chewed gum stuck to the sides of his hairless head.

He could've been made of pale dough, rolled into a ball and plucked by fingernails until he was covered with lumps and peaks. He wore a long-sleeved shirt buttoned to the collar, but his hands were covered with the growths, and I could imagine what his body must be like.

He had a peculiar odor, like he was rotting where he stood, and the smell caused me to stumble backward. He smiled, showing perfect white teeth, all that might be left after the rest of him degenerated into a bubbling pile of protoplasm.

He looked around my dim room, moving only his eyes, then stepped inside before I could say anything. The wind followed him in, blowing grit across my linoleum floor.

"All clear, Mr. Sweeney," the misshapen giant rasped, and a short, fine-boned man glided into the room past him. The giant pushed the door closed, shutting out the wind. Even in the dim light, I could see that his hand left an oily, sweaty palm print on my door. I suppressed a shudder.

I would've recognized Sultan Sweeney even if I hadn't already heard talk on the streets about his grotesque bodyguard. You couldn't live along East Central Avenue for long without crossing Sultan's path, or at least being warned away from him. He'd only been pimping girls along the Cruise for a couple of years, since arriving in town from his native New Orleans, but ruthlessness had been good for business. He wore a shiny charcoal suit worth more than my entire wardrobe.

He straightened his lapels indignantly, glaring at the door as if the wind had nearly blown off his clothes.

He ran a manicured hand over his hair, which was slicked back into a tight-fitting swim cap that framed his face.

Sultan had the face of a china doll—high, chiseled cheekbones and thin, arching eyebrows, and skin pale and creamy as yogurt. The face Michael Jackson has been paying to acquire. Sultan had come by his naturally, and it had made him a good living as the bait in a woman trap, one that led to prostitution and degradation and early death.

"I'm lookin' for Bubba Mabry. Dat you?" Sultan's tongue rolled thickly around the words, still dancing to a Bourbon Street rhythm, that peculiar mix of Dixie and Brooklyn spoken only in New Orleans.

My leg bumped my bed, and I realized I'd been edging away from the big bodyguard.

"Uh, yeah, I'm Bubba Mabry." I looked from one to the other, trying to see if being Bubba Mabry was going to get me in trouble. Again.

I couldn't read anything in the giant's lumpy face, but a hard glint behind Sultan's brown eyes made me nervous. Had I crossed him somehow? What could I have done? I'd hardly left my room for days, a prisoner of the wind.

"What's de mattah, Bubba? Somethin' wrong?"

"No, no. I just wasn't expecting company. What can I do for you?"

"You could start by offerin' me a seat."

I blurted an apology and stepped out of the way so Sultan could reach my room's one easy chair. The big chair made him look even smaller as he settled back and crossed his legs. His shoes were pointed black loafers with a pebbly surface. Alligator hide.

The giant leaned against the door, blocking any escape. He reached into a pants pocket, which made me stiffen, and pulled out a wrinkled white handkerchief. He wiped his palms on it and patted his chin

5

ever so carefully, like touching the tumid tumors would make them spread.

"I know it's hard not to stare at Hughie, Bubba, but it ain't polite." Sultan smiled up at me from the chair.

"Sorry." Hughie didn't seem offended. His ravaged face seemed incapable of much expression.

"Besides," Sultan said, "I'm de one with de bidness proposition. Pay attention to me."

I apologized again, and perched on the corner of my bed, staring at Sweeney's face to show him I was concentrating.

"What kind of business?"

"An investigation. Dat is what you do, idn't it?"

"Right, right. Sorry."

"You about the sorriest man I ever met." Sultan gave me a chilly smile. "You've apologized four or five times since we got here."

My face flushed hot, but I swallowed and muttered something about having been half asleep when they knocked.

"Well, if you're sleepin' in de daytime, I guess you got time to do some nosing around for me."

"Depends on what it's about."

Sultan's grin melted and he shot me the same hawkish glare he'd given the windstorm.

"It's about murder, Bubba. Thought you'd figured dat out by now."

"I don't know what you mean."

"My ladies, Bubba. Three of my ladies been killed. Didn't you know dat? What do you do, just sit here all day, watchin' TV?"

"I'm working on a case. I couldn't face that wind anymore so I called it a day."

He nodded, looking me over.

"Well, when you're workin' for me, a little wind better not get de best of you."

I straightened, glanced over at Hughie, and said, "I'm not working for you yet."

"Well, you gonna be. I've decided you're de man for de job."

I said nothing.

"See, I don't think much of what de police been doin'. They've been what you'd call halfhearted in tryin' to find out who's killin' my girls."

I could see a vein pumping in the milk-glass skin at his temple. Other than the movement of his lips, it was the only sign he was alive. He sat perfectly still, poised in the armchair, as conscious of his body as a cat.

Hughie sighed and shifted on his feet, getting more comfortable, accustomed to waiting. His stale breath seemed to fill the room. I tried to focus on Sultan Sweeney.

"I'm not surprised the police aren't trying very hard," I said. "They don't think much of folks on the Cruise. The more dead, the fewer they have to arrest."

Sultan lowered his chin a centimeter, which I took to be a nod.

"Since de newspapers picked it up, dey shown a little more interest. But dat's been a worse problem."

"How's that?"

"Bad publicity. The johns are scared to come down here. My girls are scared to work. I spend all my time patrollin' the street like *I'm* a cop, makin' sure everybody workin'."

I nodded, kept quiet. I didn't want any part of this case. Sultan wasn't going to like that answer.

"Besides, it's bad for me. Shows a lack of respect. We need to set an example."

I sighed, stood up, put some distance between me and Hughie. My small room wouldn't let me go far, and I turned to face them when I got to the wall. I thought of my pistol, safely locked away in the glove compartment of my car. There wasn't anything else in the room I could use for a weapon. I keep it that way because clients are always dropping by. Sometimes, very angry clients. I don't want them picking something up and whopping me with it. Now my own careful planning betrayed me.

"So you want me to finger somebody, then you'll knock him off?"

Sultan stared at me from under arched eyebrows, waiting.

"Sorry, but I don't work that way. I can't take your case."

Sultan's face hardened ever so slightly, limestone becoming marble.

"I tell you what, Bubba. You find whoever's doin' it, then we'll talk about what happens next."

I shook my head. My eyes darted between Sultan's crystal face and Hughie's lumpy one, and I tried to get them under control. Nothing looks more frightened, or shiftier, than twitching eyes.

"Is dat a 'no'?"

"Yes. I mean no. I can't take your case. There's too much heat. I try to stay out of cases the cops are working. Especially murder. It pisses them off to have private eyes poking around."

"I don't care about dat."

"I do. I have to. I've come close to losing my license before."

"Don't worry about your license."

"Let me decide what my worries are. Get yourself another boy."

Sultan gave me his cold stare for a long moment. I could feel the tension building in my shoulders.

"I tell you what you bettah worry about, Bubba. You bettah worry about Hughie. He don't like it when people sass me."

Hughie shifted slightly, ready to waddle over and wham me if Sultan blinked. The thought of being touched by him gave me the trembles.

"Whoa, now. No need to get carried away. I didn't mean any insult. But I told you, I've already got a case. It's pretty much taking up all my time."

Sultan cut his eyes ever so slightly, just enough to make me turn and look at my still-warm TV in the corner. His meaning was clear.

"What's dis case you're workin'?"

"I can't talk about it."

"What's so important you can't spare a day or two workin' for me?"

"Really, I can't say anything."

"You can tell us. Ain't dat right, Hughie?"

Hughie studied a fingernail, which looked red and infected around the quick. He tugged at it experimentally, and the thought it might be rotted enough to come loose made my stomach roil. I looked away.

"It's, uh, there's this lady, and, uh, someone stole something that belongs to her and I'm, ah, tracking it down."

"Why'n't you say so, boy? If it's just stolen merchandise, I'll replace it and you can get right on my case."

"It's irreplaceable. It's a collection."

"Of what?"

"I really can't talk about it. You know, the client's privacy, all that."

This time, he asked through a tightened jaw. "Collection of *what?*"

"Dolls. Little kewpie dolls like they used to give out at state fairs."

The ice fled Sultan's face, and he allowed himself a grin.

"You hear dat, Hughie? Man been lookin' for kewpie dolls. Well, now, I can see why you couldn't get involved in somethin' like murder right now. Busy with kewpie dolls and all."

I hung my head. Privacy be damned, this is why I didn't want to tell him. I knew I'd have to listen to this.

"What de hell kinda private eye are you?" Sultan leaned forward in his chair, and his voice was low, contemptuous. "What's de mattah? You scared to poke around de Cruise a little bit? You just wanna sit here in dis room and hide from de wind?"

My throat felt too tight to say anything. I might squeak.

Hughie's attention was back on me, his eyes menacing in that dropped pizza of a face. Sultan leaned back in the chair, exhaled, crossed his legs. He studied the snout of his alligator shoe for a second, and when he looked back up, the smolder was gone from his eyes.

"What's it gonna be, Bubba? I'm done talkin' to you."

I looked back and forth between them, and my eyes settled on Hughie's crustacean hands. They flexed ever so slightly.

"Okay, I'll do it. But I can only spare a couple of days. And if I find the killer, I'm going straight to the police."

Sultan's mouth rose a hair's breadth at one corner.

"I'll need a retainer," I said quickly, but the shadow of a smile didn't disappear like they so often do.

Sultan reached inside his suit and pulled out a roll of crisp bills. His manicured fingers peeled off two hundreds, and he tossed them on the table beside his chair. My mood brightened.

"Dat enough?"

"That's swell."

He produced a business card from another pocket and flipped it on top of the money.

"You call me every day at dat number, Bubba. Let me know how it's goin', how much it's costin' me."

I nodded, but kept my distance as he rose and Hughie gripped the doorknob.

"And Bubba, you call me when you know who done it. Don't call the police. Dis my bidness."

Hughie threw open the door, and they disappeared into the wind.

2

I poured myself a short bourbon and flopped into the big easy chair Sultan Sweeney had occupied. The seat was still warm, which surprised me. He looked cold through and through, like everything he touched should come away with a veneer of frost.

I sipped the whiskey, let its warmth work on my nerves. The money lay beside me on the table, wise old Ben Franklin smiling up smugly. It didn't do much to comfort me.

I'd just gone to work for a pimp. That was a first. Guess it was a first for him, too, because he hadn't even waited around for me to ask him questions about the murders. Names and addresses of the victims, how they were killed, nothing. Just got what he wanted, then he was gone. And I'm left maundering through my thoughts, firmly in his employ and with damned few ideas about where to begin.

I suppose Sultan figured I'd already heard all about the killings, living on the Cruise and all. And, truth to tell, I did know most everything he could've told me. Thanks to Felicia Quattlebaum, I knew plenty.

Felicia had developed a morbid fascination for the

hookers along the Cruise lately. Part of it was that the Albuquerque *Gazette* had assigned her to cover the growing controversy over the sin corridor along Central Avenue, the hot issue in the coming primary election. Another part, I suspected, was some sort of twisted jealousy. Some small secret part of her unconsciously resented the hookers and their proximity to me.

As usual with Felicia, knowledge bred opinions, and I'd heard a lot of what she thought about prostitution. Other times, I could feel her pumping me for firsthand information about life on the Cruise. There wasn't much I could tell her about the politics of it all, or about the murders that kept Felicia's stories on the front page. Naturally, she'd assume I was holding out on her, and she'd get miffed, and we'd get into another fight.

What's weird about it is that the Big Fight, the one that had become the Wall in our Relationship, as Felicia called it, was about me living down here among the criminals and hookers and crazy vagrants who thrive in the neon light of Central Avenue. She wanted me to move Uptown with her, to escape the littered streets and the piss-stink alleys, the wanton women and violent men.

No way she could stay on the Cruise, she'd said. The quick boom of the occasional stray gunshot at night made her edgy. To me, it just meant more potential clients.

But *now,* now that a Story's involved, Felicia couldn't be more interested in the Cruise, wanting to know slimy details, wanting to study with a microscope the mechanics of the place. As if she could arrange into a pattern a transient society governed by superstition and fear and sweeping, powerful randomness.

It worried me to have her cornering people on the

Cruise. Central Avenue is a place where you keep your head down. Looking the wrong way at the wrong guy can get you killed. And she's out there buttonholing bikers and chasing hookers down the street, barking questions. She, of course, saw it as chauvinism on my part. It was all right for *me* to nose around Central, turning over rocks and poking sticks into hidey-holes. But when she did it, I objected. There'd been more fights.

And now I was working for a pimp. She was going to *love* that. I'd just been telling her how I was trying to land more upscale clients, how I was chipping away at the connections I'd built up along Central Avenue. She would see working for Sultan Sweeney as a relapse. How could I make her understand I'd been forced into it by the threat in Sultan's eyes, by the silent menace of the moldering giant?

My drink was gone. I set the glass on top of the money, watched the damp ring from its bottom soak into Benjamin Franklin's face. The money was the one bright spot in all this. I desperately needed money. The bills I owed and my inability to pay them had become paralyzing, like the wind that still hammered at my window.

I tried talking to myself, to see if that would propel me from the chair.

"You can't hunker in the bunker forever, boy. The clues aren't going to come knock on your door."

I didn't twitch. I tried to think of something I could pursue by telephone. The phone sat on the nightstand, within reach. I wouldn't have to get out of my chair. Maybe I could become a famous detective who never stands up. Naw, it's been done. *Ironsides.*

The thought of the TV show made me realize I'd been staring at the blind green eye of the switched-off television. A bad habit. Before long my mind would create little patterns in the reflections there. I'd end up

14

like One-Eye Johnny over at the Mother Road Motel, a toothless old coot in a ragged T-shirt, cackling about how he's watching Sid Caesar in an empty aquarium.

I exhaled and straightened up. I had to do something to break this inertia. I snatched up the telephone and dialed Felicia's number at the Albuquerque *Gazette*. The easiest way to break the news about working for Sultan Sweeney might be over dinner, a dinner paid for with his money. A cheap dinner.

The phone rang four times, and a secretary picked it up and informed me Felicia was on another line. I agreed to hold, and was punished with Muzak.

I tried to picture who Felicia was interviewing. One of the hotheaded fundamentalists who were trying to preach away prostitution? Maybe one of the many politicians who'd taken up the crusade. At election time, politicians become more sharkish than usual. An opportunity to display righteous indignation is like blood in the water.

The debate had led to some strange bedfellows. Democrats siding with Republicans, trying not to be outdone on morality. The mayor's office racing the City Council to get into the newspapers. Even the governor, a hooting, pants-hitching rancher who talked like he had a mouthful of marbles, had a thing or two to say about what a turrible sitcheeayshun had developed along Central. Like it was something new. Like there hadn't been hookers working the streets of Albuquerque since before the railroad came West.

In a way, I thought, Felicia is part of Sultan Sweeney's problem. She'd written the stories about the killings. The front-page stories had thrown gasoline on the election fire, giving the politicians something to wail over. The creeps wouldn't give a living hooker the time of day, but a dead one was a safe cause.

Even the hookers themselves were making headlines. Some woman I didn't know, a call girl named Rosie Corona, had been trying to organize them into a political action committee. It was called SCORE, which stood for Start Coordinated Organizing and Retraining Efforts, something like that. Felicia had written stories about hookers being trained in secretarial skills (and I'd thought how popular those secretaries would be), and about how others were trying to get prostitution decriminalized, so they could work in the relative safety of brothels, like in Nevada. It seemed cross purposes to me—either get them out of the business or help them make a business of screwing —but Felicia's stories had skated past that problem. A two-pronged effort just meant more stories.

Naturally, I've become Felicia's most faithful reader. Let me give you some advice: If you know reporters, read everything they write. Hunt for their bylines, no matter how far back in the paper they might be buried. Otherwise, you get conversations like this:

"So, Sanchez denies everything."

A pregnant pause.

"Sanchez?"

"Yeah, Sanchez, the guy in my story. I finally got hold of him this afternoon."

"Oh. Right."

"He says he didn't do it."

"Uh-huh. Do you believe him?"

"I don't know. He's got a pretty good alibi. Want to guess what it is?"

Some throat-clearing.

"Well, I, uh, I haven't really given it much thought—"

"Come on, you're the private eye. Make a stab at it."

"I wouldn't have the slightest idea."

"Come on, it's *obvious.*"

"Not to me."

A change in expression, eyes going flinty.

"You know what I'm talking about, right? You read my story?"

"Uh, no. I haven't had a chance to read the paper today. I was going to get to it. It's in my car."

"Oh. Never mind. We can talk about it some other time."

"Sorry."

"No, no, that's okay. It's not like you have to read everything I write."

"I do, though."

"Uh-huh. Well, don't worry about it. It doesn't matter to me. Really."

Do yourself a favor. Read the paper.

I've always been a newspaper reader anyway. I go through the paper each day, clipping out stories about crimes and crusades and crackpots. I save them in a sloppy filing system in my dresser. My business is information. You can never tell what will come in handy.

I remembered clipping some of Felicia's stories about the murders on Central Avenue, and I made mental plans to rummage around later until I found them.

A voice came over the phone, stentorially announced the next musical number. What a job, I thought, a Muzak deejay. Enough to push you into a coma.

I was beginning to feel like I could doze off when Felicia finally came on the line, snapping, "Quattlebaum."

"Hi, it's me. Am I catching you at a bad time?"

"Yeah. Hold on a second."

The Muzak returned before I could offer to call back. I held the phone out away from my head, but that only made it worse, letting the sobbing strings fill my room rather than just leak into one ear.

I wondered whether Felicia was still mad from our last encounter. I tried to remember if we'd fought the last time we were together, and what it was about, but all the sharp-edged exchanges of the past few months blurred together. Our relationship had become one long conversation. And the topic never changed: I was ruining any chance of our having a future together by insisting on staying along the Cruise.

It began shortly after we finished the Book. Felicia stayed with me during the writing and editing, but once she didn't have that to focus on, the Cruise got the better of her.

She'd quit her job at a Florida-based supermarket tabloid to stay in Albuquerque and write the Book with me, trying to cash in on our big news event: the revelation that Elvis Presley was still alive.

We'd virtually locked ourselves in my tiny room, and the weeks had been a dream state of new intimacy and lovemaking and work, work, work. Felicia had decided it would be best if I wrote it and she edited it because I was the private eye and people liked to read that sort of thing. Then she stood over me, practically cracking a whip, while I sweated out what happened between me and her and the King of Rock 'n' Roll.

Felicia sent the Book off to an editor she knew in New York. The publishing company saw the value of getting the book out in a hurry. They cranked out thousands of paperbacks, rushed them into supermarkets and airports, and the book sank without a trace. Nobody bought it. The lurid cover and sensational claims put off serious readers. And it seemed people willing to plunk down fifty cents for a tabloid full of bogus Elvis sightings weren't willing to part with five bucks to read about the real deal.

My part of the advance money had gone to a new transmission in my twenty-year-old Chevy Nova and to the new TV that stared sightlessly from the corner.

And it had been just enough to screw up my taxes for the year. I'd sent my tax return in a month ago, with no check inside to cover the six hundred bucks I owed, and I expected to hear from the IRS any day. I just hoped I could come up with enough to cover it before they caught up to me.

My newfound notoriety locally hadn't helped my business, as we'd hoped. In fact, people seemed downright reluctant to hire a private detective who claimed to have met the living Elvis.

But we'd been doing okay back then, both of us living off Felicia's salary, and I was beginning to settle into a happy routine when Felicia announced we had to move from Central Avenue. Some wino had wagged his wanger at her on the street and, for her, that was the last straw.

I hadn't even noticed living on the Cruise was bothering her. I was so accustomed to living among trash, both inert and human, I barely noticed tattooed hookers and vomit in the gutters and leering, hopped-up bikers. But these things disturbed Felicia. Why suffer among the true grit of Central Avenue, she asked, when we can get a spick-and-span apartment just a few miles away? Carpet, dishwasher, mountain views, a laundry you can enter unarmed.

I took a look at the one she picked out, a newly decorated mauve wonder of modern convenience, but I couldn't make the move. The place is in the Northeast Heights, off Wyoming Boulevard, and it's all balconies and handrails, a four-deck ship adrift in a sea of parking lots and fast food joints and dental offices.

The place was teeming, but there were no people. Nobody walking, nothing to see. Just cars. Lots and lots of cars. The Heights is life at forty miles an hour. Everything can be had by drive-up window, including liquor. You drive to your job, the bank, the convenience store, the dry cleaners, and your feet never have to touch pavement. And here's a cold six-pack. Please don't drink and drive.

At least it's not Southern California. Not yet. I heard of a place out there that has drive-by funerals. They prop the stiff up in a window and you can blow it a kiss from your air-conditioned bucket seat. Sure, you have to slow down as you pass the window, but it's the least you can do in your hour of mourning.

"Hello, Bubba. Sorry for the wait. I finally got free."

Felicia sounded tired, phone-weary.

"Busy day?"

"Every politician in town has been calling me. Everybody wants to go on record as being against whores."

She has such a sweet way about her sometimes.

"Sounds like you've uncovered a trend."

She sighed into my ear, like she didn't have the patience to talk to one more person. Particularly me.

"Listen," I said quickly, "I got a new case today, and I thought you might like to go out to dinner tonight. On me."

"I can't. I've got to cover an anti-sin rally. Did I mention the politicos are against sin, too? The rally's over on East Central, not too far from you."

"Hmm, I haven't heard about it."

"It was in my story yesterday. Front page."

"Oh, *that* rally."

"Yeah, right. Anyway, it starts at six, so I'll be busy through dinner."

"How about after? Maybe I could see you at the rally, then we could grab a bite."

"I've got to come back here and file my story for the late edition. Besides, you wouldn't like the rally. It would make you crazy, listening to those guys insult your neighborhood."

I didn't want to touch that. I muttered something

about maybe seeing her over there anyway, and tried to get off the phone.

Before she hung up, she said, "So, you got a new case?"

"You probably need to get back to work."

"What's it about?"

"I gotta go."

"Bubba!"

"I'll tell you about it later. 'Bye."

3

Albuquerque's motto should be the Rubbernecker City. People out here believe in slowing their cars to take a look. It stems, I think, from the town's great cruising tradition. For generations, a major source of entertainment has been tooling along Central Avenue, old Route 66, in low-slung, highly polished automobiles.

Kids all over congregate that way, I guess. I remember cruising Main Street in Nazareth, Mississippi, when I was in high school, clowning for the girls and throwing beer bottles in people's yards. Teens need that constant contact, that social structure, to make certain, every second, they're still cool.

For years, Downtown, with its curbside parking and frequent stoplights, was the low-rider hangout. If you forgot and tried to drive through that area on a Saturday night, it could be a maddening hour or two until you reached the other side. Downtown merchants bitched about it until the cops cracked down on the cruisers, harassing them until they'd moved west of the Rio Grande. Now the merchants bitch that nobody comes Downtown at night.

An adolescence spent swimming in slow-moving traffic spawns rubberneckers, I suppose, because we've sure got them here. An accident in one lane of the freeway stalls traffic in all directions while everybody stops to take a gander. Naturally, dead stops on the freeway lead to more accidents and more rubbernecking and it's a wonder we ever get anywhere at all.

Anyhow, that's how I found the rally against sin. Traffic on Central was backed up thick west of San Mateo Boulevard, and I figured everyone up ahead was pausing to gawk at the holy rollers.

The young trees in the median had quit bending with the wind, but they slumped over, worn out from fighting it. A brown haze hung over the city, and you could practically hear the blown sand settling back to earth. The setting sun streaked the airborne granules with wild colors—reds, oranges, neon pinks. I practiced my patience while we putted along, our engines given a bass beat by the speakers of a throbbing Camaro. When I was still a block away, I could see the rubberneckers who'd gotten their fill roaring away up ahead. I turned onto a side street crowded with parked cars.

The rally was across Central's six lanes, but a handful of Cruise denizens loitered on the north side of the street, watching the spectacle from a safe distance, as if mingling with starched-collar church folk might taint them somehow, might make them question their own choices.

I walked among them as I picked my way to the intersection. A couple of teenage pretty boys, wearing tight cutoffs and eye makeup, puckered and preened as I passed. The rally had temporarily slowed their business. This part of Central Avenue was sometimes knee-deep in boys making their dope money by giving blow jobs to the chicken hawks who circle the block in expensive cars.

The boys siphoned business off the porn shop down the street. Men coming out of the steamy book racks and quarter-movie booths were primed for a little quick action, horny enough to overlook the gender of the person squatting between their legs.

The rally leaders had set up shop directly across from the porn shop, a windowless beige building with pink neon across the front that said NEWSWORLD. As if anyone in town thought you'd go in there to buy a newspaper or the *National Review*. It used to tickle me that the anonymous owners, with their twisted sense of humor, had equated pornography and news. But that was before I got romantic with a reporter. Now I keep those kinds of thoughts to myself.

The rally centered around a platform erected in the parking lot of a shoe repair shop. The repair shop proprietor was probably all for the crusade against prostitution. It'd be rough to watch the hustlers work outside your window every day. The platform, hammered together of fresh yellow pine lumber, had been strung with a few balloons and a red-white-and-blue streamer sashed across the front. Not too festive, though. Church folk don't want to be showy.

I crossed Central and slipped into the crowd of a couple of hundred people. I was surprised at how young they were. I guess I'd expected they'd all be dried-up old Puritans. But there were young couples and kids romping around and well-scrubbed teens whose fresh faces provided a sharp contrast to the wary-eyed chickens across the street. A few of the women raked at their hair, trying to free the tangles left by a full day of wind. Most just stared at the stage expectantly.

A lot of them wore T-shirts that said "Jesus Saves" or "God is the Pilot. I'm just along for the ride." And they carried signs that said STAMP OUT SIN or THE WAGES

OF SIN ARE DEATH or SAVE CENTRAL AVENUE FROM ITSELF. I could barely make my way through the crowd for reading. Others sported brooms they carried like protest signs, and it took me a minute before I understood they showed the Christians meant to clean up Central.

I spotted Felicia and the other reporters standing to one side of the platform, clumped together over their notebooks.

A young man with close-cropped hair and a tight suit was winding up a speech at the microphone. He seemed new to the trade, nervous being this close to real sin. The crowd applauded warmly when he managed to finish without swallowing his Adam's apple.

The rally suddenly was bathed in intense white light from two television cameras. I winced and tried to edge out of camera range. The lights made the crowd come alive. They pointed their signs at the cameras and began bouncing up and down and clapping and waving their brooms, making sure their enthusiasm would be shown on the ten o'clock news.

What is it about a television camera that causes people to lose their minds? Guy tries to do a stand-up on the evening news and there's always a bunch of kids behind him, mugging and flexing their muscles. Camera pans the crowd at a football game, and grown men go nuts, leaning over balcony rails and waving their arms and hooting, all on the off chance their friends will make out their half-inch-high faces on the home screen.

Up on the platform, a skinny little man with carefully blow-dried black hair waved a white handkerchief, beating rhythm for the chants of "No sin! Save our city!" It was all a little too orchestrated, and after a minute or two, the lights died. So did the chants, replaced by an excited tittering hubbub.

As I circled behind the reporters, I heard the TV types muttering among themselves, trying to decide if they had enough footage, whether they could bag the rest of the rally and go eat. Felicia was near the front of the dozen or so reporters, always jockeying for position because she's too short to see over her peers. I slipped in front of a tall, bearded reporter, who glared at me and said, right into Felicia's ear, "Hi. I'm here."

She jumped at the sudden voice, like God Himself might've shown up at the rally for a few words with her. Someone giggled nearby, and Felicia glared up at me through her big horn-rimmed glasses. Her eyes cut from side to side, seeing who was around us, and in that instant I could see she was embarrassed I was there. Like she was measuring which of her competitors would gain from seeing her whispering with a penniless private eye, the Elvis guy. I got a dull ache in my chest, and I realized I wasn't breathing, and I inhaled deeply to make the pain stop. It sounded enough like a sigh, I guess, that Felicia's features softened and a smile tugged at the corner of her mouth. She said, "Shh, Jericho's about to blow his horn."

She jerked her head toward the stage, and I followed it with my eyes, and we both watched as the skinny man silenced the crowd by clearing his throat into the microphone.

He made a show of patting his forehead with his hankie, and said, "It's certainly a hot one tonight, isn't it, folks? Soon as that wind died, things warmed up."

His voice had a boom that seemed to come up from the soles of his shoes. It didn't match his body, which was short and frail, the body of someone too pious to enjoy a meal. He wore a stifling black suit and a starched white shirt; his sharp-nosed face had the hard squint of a farmer. In another life he'd be a rural disc jockey, one of those who always surprises you when you meet him in person. A big voice coming out of a little man.

"Yes, the Lord gave us a nice clear night for this rally. And he threw in a little heat to remind the sinners what it's going to be like in Hell."

That got the crowd cheering, and I watched over Felicia's shoulder as she scribbled down what he'd said. She took notes in some strange mix of shorthand and abbreviations and scrawled words, and it might as well have been Egyptian hieroglyphics for all I could make out.

At the top of the page, though, in block letters, were the words REV. SKIP JERICHO, and I figured that was the scarecrow at the microphone. I recognized the name from Felicia's news stories. Jericho was a leader in the anti-prostitution crusade, and the politicians had stampeded to his door. Felicia followed, and had quoted Jericho often.

Preachers make me nervous, but Jericho started off all right. He made a few little jokes, he played to the crowd's enthusiasm, he got in a plug for his church.

"We call it Victory Chapel," he said, "because it's a church for winners. God likes winners. And He's willing to grant victory to those who give Him their all."

There was a smattering of applause, and Jericho used the break to rearrange his features. The smile slid off his face, pulling his mouth down at the corners, and his eyebrows knitted a deep furrow over his nose. Those in front saw the transformation first, and sent a hush racing to the back of the crowd.

"Now, let's talk about losers." His deep voice had changed, too, becoming angry and flat. "The losers are the ones who refuse to bend to God's will, the ones who won't play by His rules."

He gestured over the crowd, toward the people on the far side of the street.

"These people let money or sex or other worldly pleasures become their focus. They want everything now, now, now, and they don't worry about the long-term cost. They push aside the truth, which is that life is a long struggle and the victory doesn't come until the end."

A few scattered "Amens" rose up to meet Jericho, and he nodded slightly to acknowledge them. He wiped his face with the handkerchief, and his scowl deepened. His voice dropped until it was an amplified whisper breathing from the speakers.

"These losers always think they can have their victories in this life. Some even profit from the weaknesses of others—"

He waved his handkerchief at the porn shop across the street.

"—and God has reserved a special corner of Hell for them."

That got a rise out of the crowd, which hooted and applauded other people's Eternal Punishment.

"Our city has let sin thrive down here on Central Avenue. Pornographers sell their dirty books, and bars pour whiskey, and young women lose their dignity and their souls, selling the bodies God has given them."

Nodding and concerned muttering from the crowd, right on cue.

"We citizens have ignored it. We go to our houses in other parts of town, and we stay away from Central. We ignore what's going on down here, what's happening to our young people.

"That's what people did in Sodom and Gomorrah. They ignored the sinfulness, until it spread like a cancer through both cities, until it was too late to stop it. And you all remember what happened to Sodom and Gomorrah. God rained fire on them."

I spotted a wide-eyed little girl who clutched at her mother's skirt, terrified at what God had wrought. Years of nightmares to come, I thought, just because Mommy believed someone named Skip Jericho could actually stop sin along Central. Or anywhere else.

"There are ways to stop it," he said, like he was reading my thoughts. "We have to show the mayor and the City Council we won't stand for it anymore. Central Avenue runs through our fair city like a dark blot, the way the river makes a black strip in the city lights at night. It's up to us to shine God's cleansing light down here."

A cheer rose from the multitudes, and Jericho waved and stepped back from the microphone. A few of the women in front had tears in their eyes. All were flushed with love and zeal and righteousness. It occurred to me they probably all were members of Jericho's congregation, the vanguard of his crusade. And I thought about how few people it took, if they were dedicated, to change the city's mind about things.

Jericho introduced the next speaker, a city councilman named Quentin Dudley, who was at the microphone by the time I started paying attention again. Dudley had a tough act to follow, and seemed to know it. He read quickly and mechanically off a page.

Dudley was a contrast in build, too, standing tall and muscular inside his summer-weight suit. He had cropped blond hair and a thick neck and a square jaw. His eyes were a little close-set, which gave him an air of stupidity he'd somehow overcome.

His speech consisted of automatic things about how the council always wants to know what the citizenry is thinking, and how he appreciated the efforts of those at the rally and how much he'd like to have their vote on Tuesday. I had pretty much tuned him out when he said something that pricked up my ears.

"You know, it's not just pornography and prostitution we're talking about here. It's murder."

He wasn't referring to his notes anymore. Maybe he figured he needed to liven it up after Jericho's mini-sermon.

"Several prostitutes have been killed along Central Avenue recently. Some of you might think that's the way God intended those people to go, but the fact is we've got a district here where it goes on all the time. Because we've let Central Avenue get so bad, it's like a magnet to the prostitutes and the criminals and the killers. You put all the bad people in one place, and they're going to start killing each other."

My neck got hot as anger crept up from my chest. What about the *good* people who live down here? What about the ones too poor to live anywhere else? What about people like me, who *choose* it?

I made a sound, between a grumble and a growl, and Felicia shot me a look over her shoulder. She cocked an eyebrow, as if to say, "I told you so," and I shut up and looked away.

These people didn't understand the Cruise. Dudley was from the Heights. Felicia might even live in his district. And, like her, he couldn't see past the dirt and the sin and the crime statistics when he looked at life down here.

Every city needs an area for transients, especially a city like Albuquerque, an urban oasis at the crossroads of two interstate highways, plunked down in the middle of freaking nowhere. People move—geographically, socially, economically. There's got to be somewhere for them to live while they're bringing themselves up from the fringes of society. Sure, it's going to be a tough place. They're tough people. But if there's nowhere for them to go, eventually they're going to start bedding down in your living room, and they'll be too tough, or you'll be too soft, to do anything about it.

Within this transient society, things happen at a faster clip. Friendships form and dissolve, romances last one night, strangers kill each other. Transient people are like pinballs, bouncing from one location/situation/addiction/relationship/job to another until they find a place they fit. Some never fit. Some never try. Some never get a chance to fit before they're taken from the game. And it all happens so fast, they're never really sure what happens next. They're moved by forces beyond their control, governed only by the laws of nature and by chaos.

The trick, then, is to watch it from up close. If you get close enough, and squint just right, you can see most anything. You can see the subtle, tremulous strata of the society, the rapid rise and fall of human lives. A person's position on the Cruise can change overnight with the good fortune of meeting the right person or scoring some dough. If the luck really hits, they'll disappear from the Cruise, never looking back. But it can go the other way just as randomly, resulting in a slow slide or sudden death. The trips down the escalator are the only ones you'll read about in the newspaper, the only ones you'll see from the Heights.

By the time I tuned in again, Dudley was done, and was offering his wife, Marilyn, the microphone. Marilyn looked very prim in a navy-blue knit suit, dark stockings, and low heels. Long black hair framed her pale face and emphasized her skinny neck. Her eyes bulged a little, so that she looked startled or frightened all the time. Maybe she was.

"Thank you, Quentin," she chirped in a shrill little voice. It was a voice I knew I couldn't listen to for long.

"I would like to speak to you from the perspective of a woman," she tweeted. "Women get exploited in every way down here on Central Avenue."

Central was still filled with slow-moving cars, and tires squealed and a car honked and someone shouted loud enough that heads turned in the crowd.

The mumble that rippled through the audience made Marilyn Dudley go even more rigid and frigid than before. She cleared her throat and rattled the papers in her hands.

"Now I'm no feminist," she continued. Felicia glanced back at me and rolled her eyes. "But I'm against the degradation of these women through pornography and prostitution and even murder. The women of Albuquerque must stand up for themselves, and for women everywhere, by putting a stop to the sin on Central Avenue."

That got some applause, more than her husband had gotten, anyway, and you could see it fill her with confidence.

Then a hoarse shout came from the back of the crowd, "Hey, baby!"

Marilyn's head jerked at the sound, like someone had slapped her, and a warm blush flooded her cheeks.

Heads snapped around to glare toward Central Avenue. I stood on my toes as the cars parted and saw a drunk tottering at the far curb. He looked like a pile of old clothes. Battered shoes topped by baggy jeans and a faded lumberjack shirt hanging loose. He was standing just outside the wooden fence that screened the entrance of the porn shop from the street. He glanced back over his shoulder toward the door, like he'd just been thrown out of there, then wheeled back toward the street. The sudden pivot made him lose his balance, and he teetered just long enough that it looked like he might fall into traffic. Then he caught himself and staggered backward a step.

The crowd muttered and some of the women automatically dropped their hands over their children's eyes. Most of the heads slowly swiveled back toward the stage.

Marilyn Dudley fidgeted and cleared her throat. "As I was saying—"

"Hey, baby!" The whiskery drunk grinned across the street.

Marilyn's head drooped, she was so mortified, but she gave it one more try.

"The women of this city—"

"Hey!"

The heads turned back and forth, like the crowd was at Wimbledon. It was Marilyn's serve, but she didn't look like she could deliver. Her face was crimson.

Quentin Dudley stepped over to his wife, tried to put his arm around her. She shrugged him away and her back went stiff and she looked up at the crowd.

"It's all right, dear. I'm fine." Quentin took a step back, not sure what to do. "I'd like to finish," Marilyn said.

The crowd murmured appreciatively. Felicia scrawled furiously, flipping page after page of her notebook. The others around her did the same, and I felt conspicuous, empty-handed.

All eyes were on Marilyn Dudley. She took a deep breath, straightened the papers in her hands.

"It's nearly election day, as you all know—"

"Hey, *baby!*"

Marilyn's chin snapped and she glared over the crowd at the weaving, grinning drunk.

"What?!" she screamed. "What do you *want?*"

Everyone for three square blocks froze in place. The

sudden scream reverberated off buildings and rattled windows and straightened spines.

No one was more surprised than the drunk, who stumbled backward until a wall caught him. The shock slid off his face, and he looked down and patted the wall like an old friend who'd done him a favor. When he looked up again, the grin was back.

"I want *you,* baby!"

The crowd huffed indignantly, and the men scowled and the women frowned. This was getting to be too much.

"I want you to sit on my face! Ha-ha-ha-ha-ha."

The mothers moved their hands from their children's eyes to their ears. The children looked bewildered.

The drunk pushed himself off the wall. He grabbed the crotch of his baggy jeans and yanked it around, like he was looking for something in there.

"I want you to turn my crank!"

He laughed some more, staggered around in a circle. A grimy hand clutched at his butt as he bent over, and he waggled the sagging denim toward the Christians.

"I want you to kiss my ass!"

A couple of young men in tight jeans and bulging polo shirts detached themselves from the crowd and moved toward the drunk, but they couldn't get through the traffic, and the drunk continued his awkward jig on the far side of the stream of cars. Some of the street people who'd gathered on either side of the dancing drunk saw the clean-cut Christians headed their way, and they edged away.

"I want you to lick my dick!"

The drunk snaked out his red tongue to show her what he meant. Marilyn still stood burning on the deck, her eyes on her shoes.

Two more young lions made their way to the curb,

and the four of them pounced through a gap in the traffic and sprinted toward the drunk.

"Hey!" He stumbled backward when he saw them, tried to run, but his coordination had long since fled the country and he couldn't make his legs work.

"Hey!"

Once they reached him, the Christians didn't know quite what to do. They circled him, and he wheeled around and yelled boozily into their faces, "Don't touch me, you motherfuckers! Stay back!"

I caught movement on the stage out of the corner of my eye. Reverend Skip Jericho snatched the microphone off its stand and boomed into it, "Let's drown out this noise, my children!"

The congregation spun at his voice, and he began to sing: "Bringing in the sheaves, bringing in the sheaves . . ."

Guess that was the first song to pop into his head once he'd broken the trance the rest of us were in. It was a hymn everyone knew, and the Jericho devotees lifted up their voices in song.

"We shall come rejoicing, bringing in the sheaves . . ."

Others in the crowd were more reluctant to give up the spectacle across the street, where the four strapping men had finally figured it out and had grabbed the drunk by the arms.

"Get your fuckin' hands off me!"

The hymn did make it harder to hear the scuffle as the drunk fell against his captors and yanked his arms around. He grunted and shouted obscenities as they dragged him down the street.

"Bringing in the sheaves . . ."

Realizing he was lost, the drunk gave up fighting and turned his head to shout back over his shoulder toward the stage.

"I don't care! I don't care!"

"Bringing in the sheaves . . ."

"I still love you, baby!"

The reporters around me tried not to laugh. The congregation sang even louder, determined to defeat the Devil with decibels.

The goons disappeared around a corner with the drunk, and we didn't hear anything more from him. I glanced around at the TV cameras to see who would follow. But the cameras were pointed at the stage, and I saw no one cared what became of the drunk. I turned to find the scene I knew would be the one they'd show on the news, the picture that would make tomorrow's front page.

Quentin and Marilyn Dudley stood to Jericho's right, arms around each other, their all-American faces beaming with song. They towered over the little preacher, who clutched his handkerchief to his forehead as he sang into the microphone with all his might. Someone had handed Quentin Dudley a sign on a stick, and he waved it triumphantly at the crowd.

The sign said CLEAN UP SIN-TRAL AVENUE.

4

The congregation kept bringing in those sheaves, over and over, until I thought my head would explode. Some women instinctively slipped into hymn-voice— that dry, flat singsong that sounds like you're holding your nose. The monotonal edge spread through the crowd until they all were doing it, mesmerized, chanting their mantra.

I felt a little dizzy. I closed my eyes, and I was back at the Antioch Rock Baptist Church in Nazareth, Mississippi. The wild-eyed preacher and his hypnotic handkerchief. The punishing uncushioned pews. And those dried-up old crones in every row, whining at the top of their lungs for Salvation, their hearing aids safely turned off.

I spent every Sunday of my childhood squirming through those services, drawing glares from my devout mother, keeping my father awake. Until they ostracized Mama, then we gradually stopped going. We tried other churches, but they didn't feel right to Mama, all the people staring, and she ended up doing all her praying and Bible-reading at home.

My mother, Eloise Cutwaller Mabry, was visited by Jesus every week or two for nearly a year, starting in the fall of 1967. She sat at the kitchen table every night until all hours, after the rest of the house was silent and asleep, awaiting Jesus. He'd show up at the back door, and Mama would feed him and listen to his fractured parables. Then he'd disappear into the piney woods.

Mama was a celebrity at first, on TV and in supermarket tabloids. But resentment got the better of the town, and celebrity turned to curiosity and pride melted into embarrassment.

Then the sheriff caught Jesus. The official investigation found that Jesus was a hippie wild man, living in the woods, his brain circuitry blown. My mother refused to believe it, and Jesus didn't stick around to sort it out for her. As soon as the judge freed him on his own recognizance, Jesus vanished.

My mother's stalwart resolve about the visitations made people talk about the infamous death of her father, Pincus Cutwaller, who'd plummeted from a New York hotel window during the radio broadcast of "War of the Worlds." My grandfather had gone to New York to receive an inventors' award. He was a naturally curious man, Mama always said, and had probably been leaning out the window to marvel at spaceships and ray guns when he fell. Of course, most people believed he panicked at the news of a Martian invasion and flung himself out the window in fear.

Such a tragedy properly should be forgotten before long, but his widow, my grandmother, kept it fresh in people's minds. Every day, from the day he died until she passed away thirty years later, she wore heavy black galoshes and a rain hat. When people would mention it hadn't rained in weeks, she'd smile primly and say, "You can never tell what's going to fall from the sky."

People started to mutter, "What *is* it with these Cutwallers?" Bullies made jokes and girls giggled and it was tough, growing up under that cloud, being the last in the Cutwaller line.

I'd become a private eye largely because I feared I'd inherited some sort of sucker gene. Being a detective constantly tested whether I was falling victim to the Cutwaller credulity. I'd done all right for a long time. Barely scraping by, but not getting duped often. Then there'd been that Elvis business.

I blinked back to the present, feeling woozy, just as Felicia closed her notebook. She looked over her shoulder like she was surprised I was still there, and said, "Well, nice seeing you. I've got to hurry back and file this story."

After suffering through the rally and all the memories, I wasn't willing to just let her go. I trailed behind her as she walked to her car, and we made plans to meet for a late supper after she was done.

The crowd was breaking up. Flushed Christians, feeling good about themselves, strolled back to their cars, on their way to get ice cream for the kids. And the only difference on Central Avenue was the traffic had picked up speed again.

A few followers handed out religious tracts, and I skirted the block to avoid them. I circled an hourly rate motel to get to the side street where the Christian youth had hustled away the drunk. There was no sign of him, no blood on the sidewalk. They probably took him away somewhere, I thought. Probably had him on his knees by now, sober and praying for forgiveness.

I drove along the Cruise for a while, just killing time until I could meet Felicia at the restaurant. The sidewalks were busy with diners and winos, hookers and joggers. As it grew darker, the neon glowed brightly, creating a low-rent Las Vegas of saloons and discos, fast food places and Indian jewelry shops. Even the shoe repair shop has a neon sign on Route 66.

After an hour, I turned up Carlisle Boulevard for a long, red-light-studded cruise north. The restaurant was halfway between my part of town and the newspaper building at the north end. Felicia and I find the restaurant to be a more-or-less happy medium, though we can't understand anything the waitresses say.

It's a Chinese joint called Kung Food, and it's decorated with posters of snarling Bruce Lee and his flying fists of fury. There are the usual tinfoil dragons and bulbous paper lamp shades, but it's the martial arts stuff that sticks in your mind.

Felicia wasn't there, but I went on inside and ordered some egg rolls and hot tea. The waitress jabbered and smiled and bobbed her head, and I had no idea if she'd understood what I wanted. A few minutes later Felicia blew through the door, out of breath, and flopped into the booth opposite me.

Her chin-length brown hair was mussed and tangled. Her big glasses had slipped down her nose and she had a smear of cigarette ash on her shirtfront.

"Hi there."

"Hi. You look beat."

She exhaled toward the ceiling and raked her fingers through her hair.

"I am. I had to crank that story out in a hurry to make deadline, and that idiot Whitworth stood over me the whole time."

Whitworth was the city editor at the *Gazette,* and he and Felicia seemed to have the sort of personality conflict that would last a lifetime. I hadn't met Whitworth, but Felicia described him as a sneering lout who gave her trouble because she'd worked at a supermarket tabloid. So not only had she been forced to readjust to a daily newspaper's pace, but she'd felt she had to prove something to Whitworth and his ilk.

She'd been working a lot of long hours, she'd been on the front page nearly every day, and still this Whitworth badgered her.

Felicia pulled her feet up to sit cross-legged. She's so short her feet don't reach the floor from most grown-up chairs, and she's grown accustomed to eating from the half-lotus position.

The waitress returned and—surprise!—brought the egg rolls and tea I'd ordered. Felicia scanned a menu. I busied myself with pouring tea and arranging the little plates.

"Moo shu pork and Szechwan chicken okay with you?"

"Sure."

Felicia handed the menus to the waitress without a glance, and the waitress, looking bewildered, wandered back toward the kitchen. I wondered what food she'd bring. Probably chicken feet and pig lips.

"So," I said. "Haven't seen much of you lately. How've you been?"

"Oh, about the same. Working all the time."

That wasn't the answer I was looking for. What I really wanted to ask was: Are you still mad at me? Have we made up? I just wanted peace. If we had to live apart, me on Central and her Uptown, that was fine by me. Living together eventually brought up the Marriage Question, and I was in no hurry to reach that plateau of argument. But Felicia felt our relationship had moved backward because we'd lost the intimacy of daily contact. Once you've lived together, living apart feels halfhearted.

We'd hit that awkward stage in a relationship where it could go either way, constantly analyzing our feelings and trying to decide whether the love we felt was worth the grief we caused each other.

Sometimes, when we hadn't seen each other for a few days, she'd leave it alone and we could have some fun and remember that we were in love. But it was always simmering there, just below the surface, and it didn't take much to heat her up to the boiling point. The result was that I constantly took her temperature.

"I can see why you'd be worn-out," I said, "listening to those fundamentalists all the time."

She grinned.

"It is an earful, isn't it? And I get it all day long. Reverend Jericho gave my name and phone number out to his congregation. They've all been doing their part to get the Godless Media involved in their crusade."

"Lovely."

"Yeah. And you should see the letters. They're stuffed full of religious tracts, and there's lots of underlining and exclamation points."

"Fanatics."

"Exactly. And fanatics always give you the best quotes. They spend so much time planning what they're going to say."

I'd long ago learned Felicia, like most reporters, I guess, measured everybody and every incident by how the story would read in the newspaper. Always studying the scene, looking for an angle. It's a cynical way of looking at the world, but I guess it helps them tolerate the company they have to keep: politicians and preachers, cops and robbers, victims, villains, and each other.

"So what about you?" Felicia said. "You got a new case, huh?"

I hadn't wanted to get to that right away. I'd wanted to feel Felicia out some more first, test her mood.

"Yeah, but I'm not too happy about it."

"How come?"

"I don't think much of my client."

"Who's the client?"

"You don't want to know."

The slightest hint of evasion, and Felicia's brown eyes glitter and her questions get a sharper edge. Being stalked makes me jittery, and I get terribly careful about my answers, and pretty soon our conversation slows to the pace of a chess match.

"Don't make me worm it out of you."

I knew she could. I'd given up trying to keep my confidential investigations secret from her.

"Ah, hell, it's this guy named Sultan Sweeney. You've probably never heard of him."

"Sultan Sweeney the *pimp?*"

She'd heard of him. "Yeah. How do you know about him?"

"He's the one who'd been pimping the women who were killed. The cops can't pin anything on him, can't even prove any connection to the women, so my editors won't let me print it. As far as the *Gazette* is concerned, Sultan Sweeney is just another law-abiding citizen who could sue us."

I knew better than to let her get wound up on this topic. At the tabloid, getting sued for libel was a badge of honor. It had been hard for Felicia to adjust to the caution that cripples most dailies these days.

"Well, Sultan wants me to investigate the murders. I didn't want to do it, but he had this—this big—this *guy* with him, and it didn't seem prudent to argue."

"Jesus, Bubba, a pimp. I mean, I know you haven't had many cases come your way lately—"

"That's right. I haven't. And I can't really afford to turn one down, no matter who the client is."

"Yeah, but a pimp. That gives me the crawlies."

"Sorry, but that's the way it is. His retainer is paying for this meal."

Felicia had just taken a bite of egg roll, and she made a face like it suddenly tasted bad.

The waitress arrived with—miracle of miracles!— the right order, and the steaming platters meant it was too late for Felicia to refuse to eat on moral grounds. She spooned rice onto her plate and started shoveling the chopped vegetables and spicy chicken over it. I filled a thin pancake with moo shu pork, added a dollop of sweet plum sauce, then folded and rolled it into a neat package. Moo shu pork, the Chinese enchilada.

I like ordering it because it's nearly impossible to eat with chopsticks. You have to use a fork, which suits me fine. Felicia is so much more adept with chopsticks that she always gets the lion's share of the food when we use them. She's a voracious eater, though none of it ever shows up around her waist. Not that she's a fitness nut. Just a high-strung smoker who never gains a pound.

"You know," she said through a mouthful of food, "since I've been doing these stories, I've gained some sympathy for the prostitutes. Mostly, they're just women who've fallen on hard times or have a drug habit or something like that."

Here we go again. She swallowed, speared the next forkful.

"But pimps, they're the lowest. They don't do anything for their money but exploit other people. They're like slave owners."

"I know. I feel the same way."

"And from what I've heard about Sultan Sweeney, he's the worst of the lot. You'd better be careful around him, Bubba."

"I'm always careful."

"Not always."

I let that go, and stuffed some more food in my face. They bring you enough for four or five people, and it's a race to wolf it down before it becomes cold leftovers.

"You know, it might be a good thing you're investigating the murders," Felicia said after a moment's rumination. "If you uncover anything, it would make a good story for me."

I sighed, swallowed, and said, "You know I don't like to be in the papers."

"Could be good for business. You need the publicity."

"That's what you said about the Elvis book."

"Okay, all right, don't start rubbing my nose in that again."

I threw up my hands and shook my head, backing off. It's tough carrying on a romance with someone as touchy as Felicia.

She stewed for a while as we ate in silence. Finally, it got to me, and I said, "If you know about Sultan Sweeney, maybe you know more about the murders than the paper's been running. *You* could help *me* out."

A smile danced at the corners of her mouth. "And why would I want to do that?"

"Because I need all the help I can get."

"Too bad, Bubba." Grinning now. "Why should I help you get all the glory if you won't give me first crack at the story?"

"That's different."

"No, it's not."

"Sure it is."

"How is it different?"

"Well . . ." I wasn't even sure what we were arguing about. Felicia was always leaving me behind in these things. Was she laying a trap for me? Was this one of those political correctness tests I always failed? Would the wrong answer get me a lecture on equality or sharing or self-esteem?

"See," she said, cutting in because I was slow, "just like any other profession, journalism is a scratch-my-back-I'll-scratch-yours proposition. It's not fair to expect help from me, then turn around and tell me you don't want to be in the paper."

She got that restrained tone, like you'd use on a retarded person. Slowly explaining everything in clear terms.

"I know that," I said, a little sharply. "But I don't have anything to scratch your back with, at least not yet. I haven't even started working on the case."

Felicia was still forking Chinese food into her mouth like she was pitching hay into a loft. No amount of argument, little or big, I'd found, could interrupt her eating. She swallowed and chased it with a sip of water. Then she smiled.

"*I've* been working on it for weeks. And I've developed some pretty interesting theories, too."

"Yeah? And?"

"And maybe we'll just see who sorts it out first. I know I've got a head start, but you're a professional private investigator, after all. You can catch up on your own."

"What is this? A bet?"

"Something like that."

"What are the stakes?"

"How about professional pride?"

She was really yanking my chain now. I got a grip on myself, laughed it off and said, "Well, we'll just see, then."

She laughed, too, and the tension rose from the table.

"I knew this was coming, you know," she said.

"What?"

"I knew you'd end up investigating the killings."

"How? I didn't even know it till this afternoon."

"I know you. You've sounded restless on the phone. I knew it was driving you crazy to stand by while somebody murdered hookers in your own backyard."

This was coming dangerously close to the Big

Argument, the reasons I stayed on Central Avenue. I tried to tiptoe away.

"Nobody was paying me to do it. That's all."

"Uh-huh."

"Really. I had no interest in solving the murders until I saw the two hundred bucks Sultan Sweeney was waving around."

"You read too many detective novels, Bubba. They make you think you're tough. Sometimes, I think I know you better than you know yourself."

"Oh, yeah? You might be fooled. Nobody knows what goes on in somebody else's head."

"All I'm saying is, I knew you'd end up embroiled in this murder case. And it turns out I'm right."

God, she could get under my skin. At times like these, I had to wonder what I was doing mixed up with a person whose job is to be abrasive.

"Okay, I'll tell you what," I said. "You go on about your little investigation, and I'll do my job, and we'll see who ends up solving it first."

"Fine."

That settled, we fell into silence, mopping up the last of the meal. Neither of us wanted to say more about the killings, afraid we might give something away. Felicia watched me with twinkling eyes.

"This is going to be fun," she said.

All I could think was: what if Sultan Sweeney knew I was playing these kinds of games with a newspaper reporter? Then suddenly it was like I could smell Hughie's decay all over again, and I set down my fork.

Felicia said, "You okay?"

"Sure. Why wouldn't I be?"

"I thought maybe you were having second thoughts about our little challenge. Nervous?"

"Nah. I've never been better."

"Good."

I paid the waitress and we wandered out to our cars.

The cabbage and peppers weren't settling well in my stomach, and I trailed along behind, burping into my fist. Not the most romantic sight, and I was hoping for a little romance. It had been two weeks since we'd made love. Felicia worked late all the time. And when we were together, we spent all our time talking.

But it was late, and Felicia was tired, and I had to settle for a long kiss in the parking lot. Then we got into our separate cars and drove away to our separate homes.

When I arrived at the Desert Breeze Motor Inn, where I live, I stopped by the lobby to see the owner, Bharat "Bongo" Patel. Don't ask how he got his nickname. He flashed a brilliant smile when I came through the door.

"Ah, Meestah Bubba! Good evening. And how are you doing tonight, my friend?"

"I'm fine, Bongo. Any messages for me?"

"No. It has been a very quiet night. Business is very slow." I had figured as much, since I could see the brushes and tins of shoe polish on the floor behind him. Bongo's black dress shoes sat among them, gleaming like onyx. "But there is no business like shoe business."

"What?"

"Meestah Bubba, I am making the joke, please."

"Oh, right. That's a good one. Well, good night."

I make a point of keeping track of Bongo and his family, and the goings-on around the Desert Breeze. When there's trouble, Bongo knows I'm handy and I have a gun. He doesn't pay me for this neighborly service, but my rent hasn't gone up in ten years.

Bongo had come for me that Monday night two weeks earlier, when we'd found the corpse. I'd been asleep when he knocked, and the whole thing had seemed unreal, fuzzy around the edges.

I stumbled to my feet, my unbuttoned shirt hanging

48

loose, and snatched open the door. Bongo danced around outside like someone had given him a hotfoot.

"Meestah Bubba. Come quick!"

I used my hand to shield my eyes from the naked yellow porch lights that glare outside each room at the Desert Breeze. The pink archways along the terrace glowed orange in the light, an eerie backdrop to Bongo's skittish performance.

"Come quickly, please, Meestah Bubba! And bring your gun!"

"What's the matter?"

"I have no idea, my friend, but I have heard a very terrible thing. You will come look now, please?"

His hands darted about like black spiders.

My gun was locked in my glove compartment, and I found my keys and dug around in the Chevy until I came up with it. Bongo pranced beside my car, jabbering.

"Someone called and began telling me they heard a very loud noise in Room 102, so I am going down there to knock on the door. But before I am able to knock, I hear this terrible noise."

I grunted to my feet and slammed the car door. Bongo glanced over his shoulder in the direction of the room, tucked into the corner at the far end of the L-shaped motel.

"What did you hear?"

"It was like somebody was crying, like a little baby crying, but very low, very loud. I do not know what it was that I was hearing."

Bongo's hands snatched at his clothes, trying to pull them tight around him to protect him from whatever he'd heard.

"So you didn't knock?"

"Sheet, no, Meestah Bubba. I came for you."

We tracked off down the sidewalk, me still in my sock feet, until we reached Room 102. We stood outside the door, braced to run, listening intently, hearing nothing.

I motioned for Bongo to unlock the door. I cocked my pistol and pointed it aloft. Bongo turned the key ever so gently, holding it at arm's length, ready to flee.

I turned the knob and sprang through the door, swinging the gun around. The only person in the room was lying across the bed, her naked legs tangled in the sheets. She wore nothing but white cotton panties, the kind a little girl would wear.

I snapped back to the present and found myself standing outside the door to my room, my keys limp in my hand. Moths flitted around the specked yellow bulb, hammering the supposedly bug-proof light. It was as if they were attracted to the light but repelled at the same time, banging their heads against the bulb then staggering away to recuperate and ask themselves why they keep doing that.

Below the light, transparent packing tape shimmered on the wall. It held my business card, my only advertising besides the yellow pages. The card says "Wilton 'Bubba' Mabry, Confidential Investigations, Central Avenue." I stared at it, my professional emblem, my shingle, and knew exactly how those bugs felt.

I unlocked the door and went inside to pour myself a bourbon.

My hands were shaky, and the whiskey didn't sit well. For a moment I had been back in that room with the pretty, young corpse, her face like a baby's, her neck twisted like a purple rope. I fought to keep from blinking, afraid that closing my eyes, even for an instant, would bring the image back.

Deena had appeared in my dreams like that, lying across the bed limply, one hand trailing off the edge, her hair a tangled fan behind her. The bed had seemed to float in my nightmares, rocking gently in the breeze that blew through the open window.

I'd start awake and kick away the sweaty sheets. Then I'd take deep breaths and listen to my heart slow down, and tell myself nightmares were a normal reaction to finding a murdered corpse. My brain eventually would accept it, would file it away with the other dead people I'd seen over the years. Finding bodies is a hazard of living on the Cruise. You learn to adjust, or you go crazy. Or you pack up your stuff and move someplace where murder is an oddity, something that only happens to bad people. A place where freckled children frolic on green lawns and people brake for animals and a prostitute is something you see on *Sixty Minutes*.

I poured myself another drink.

5

I awoke early the next morning, a hangover beating a steady samba in my temples. Nothing two cups of coffee and three aspirin couldn't cure, however, and I was soon in the shower, washing away old memories and yesterday's sweat. I shaved, then spent ten minutes in front of the mirror combing my thinning brown hair, trying to cover the bare spots.

I hummed to myself as I selected clean jeans and a blue shirt from my closet. It felt good to have work to do, to be getting an early start on it. If Felicia wanted to play her little games, maybe I'd just rush right out and solve the murders. Teach her a lesson. And maybe get the dreams of Deena to flee my mind.

My first stop was the headquarters of the Albuquerque Police Department. I found a parking space by a curb meter on Tijeras Avenue, plugged in a quarter, and crossed Civic Plaza to reach the entrance to the six-story bunker. Civic Plaza deserves its place in the center of Downtown, truly representative of the Downtown scene with its acres of concrete, withering imported shrubs, and chunky gray fountain, all overseen by quirky postmodern government buildings and the peaked roofs of the two Albuquerque Plaza towers.

I waited in the tiny, video-monitored lobby of the police station while a uniformed guard phoned Homicide and made sure it was okay for me to go upstairs. My old pal Steve Romero must've agreed, because the guard gave me a visitor's badge and jerked his head toward the elevators.

Romero sat at his desk, munching an egg burrito. I could smell the green chile from across the cluttered room. The aroma made my stomach quiver, but I swallowed the hangover bile and weaved between empty desks to reach him.

It figured Romero was the first one at the office. He was probably the last to leave at night, too. The Homicide lieutenant is the one guy in the APD I respect. I've let my admiration show in the past, and I think that's why he's always nice to me. Or as nice as a cop can be. It's hard for them to come down from their daily level of irritability. They take it out on most anyone who crosses them. Sick humor and cussing and chest-thumping. Most cops are rough old boys, and their offices tend to sound—and smell— like locker rooms.

Romero is bigger than all that. He's quiet and strong and, well, shit, dignified. Whenever I'm around him, I always feel loose-jointed and goofy and more gullible than ever.

His desk sagged under the weight of the thick files and wire baskets of reports that covered all but the narrow space in the center. Just room enough for Romero's breakfast and his elbows. I sat on a hard chair beside his desk and said my hellos.

He wagged the burrito at me like a limp penis and said, "Bite?"

"No, thanks. I love chile, but never before lunch-time."

"That's because you're always hung over in the morning."

"Not always." I felt a little green around the gills, and I wondered if it showed. I'd read enough Sherlock Holmes to know a deductive mind like Romero's could pick up any little signal. I work hard to observe that well myself, but I've never been lightning-quick about it like Romero. Usually, by the time I figure out I'm about to step in shit, it's time to clean my shoe.

"So what's going on that you're down here so early in the day? I thought you private eyes slept till noon."

"Well, you know what they say about the early bird and the worm. I think you and I are hunting the same worm."

"What's that supposed to mean?"

"I've been hired to look into the killings of those hookers."

"Is that so? I'd be interested in who might want to hire you for that."

"I knew you would be, but you know I can't say. I probably wouldn't tell you if I could. I'm not too proud of it."

Romero watched me from underneath his eye-brows, then a grin split his square face.

"Sultan Sweeney? You're working for a pimp?"

I don't know why I don't just write my secrets on my face with a Magic Marker.

"Now, I didn't say that. You're welcome to make all the guesses you want. I'm not saying anything."

Romero chuckled and shook his head. The burrito had to be getting cold in his hand, but he seemed to have forgotten about it. I wished he would go ahead and finish it so I wouldn't have to smell the damned thing.

"I know times must be hard after that Elvis business," he said, "but I didn't think you'd ever end up working for a pimp."

I said nothing, but I could feel my ears burning.

Romero scowled at the cold food in his hand, dumped it onto the foil it had come in, wadded it up and tossed it in the trash. The disposal did nothing to rid the air of the chile stench. I felt queasy, uneasy.

When he turned back to me, Romero said, "You know Sweeney's a prime suspect in those killings, Bubba. He might just be keeping his girls in line."

"I heard you guys don't have anything on him, that you can't even bust him for pimping."

"Where'd you hear that?"

"I can't say."

Romero studied me some more, and it felt like my face was melting before his gaze.

"Some things never change, eh, Bubba? Here you are again, trying to get information from me, but not willing to give me anything in return."

"I know it must seem like that—"

"Because it *is* like that. Always. I don't know why I ever help you with anything."

I struggled to come up with a plausible answer, and finally said, "Maybe it's because you know the more people snooping around, the more likely something will break."

"I'm not sure I agree with that," he said. "Most cops think private eyes are just publicity-seekers who get in the way."

"You're not most cops."

Romero shrugged, inclined his head toward me, like he couldn't argue with a compliment.

"Look, all I want is whatever you've given the newspapers. I've got those clippings somewhere, but I thought I'd get a more complete picture from you."

"But you've got a contact at the *Gazette* now, don't you? How's that going?"

"Don't ask."

"That's too bad, Bubba. You need a good woman to shape you up."

"Think I need shaping up?"

"I always have."

"So you just play along with me, waiting to see if I get my act together?"

"Something like that."

"I appreciate you being so understanding." I couldn't keep the sarcasm out of my tone, even though I needed something from him.

"Don't mention it."

He leaned back in his swivel chair, laced his fingers across his wide chest, and let the grin spread across his face. No sense trying to bullshit this guy, I thought, he gets too much of it every day from people on the street, from the other cops who occupy these empty, battered desks.

Just as I was working up to whining, he sat forward suddenly and said, "Okay, Bubba, here it is."

He gave it to me fast and straight, so fast I barely kept up taking notes. He spun it all out from his head: dates, details, descriptions. It was like Evelyn Wood reading the files on his desk aloud.

"The first murder occurred around three o'clock the morning of March thirteenth at a roach palace called the Conquistador Motor Lodge. You know the place? The victim was a Hispanic male named Felix Rodriguez, aged twenty-four, five-foot-five, a hundred and forty pounds."

"Wait a minute. I'm talking about the hookers, not some guy."

"Ah, but Felix was a hooker. See, you come in here thinking about the three girls of Sultan's who've been killed. But you don't know the whole story. There've been four murders on East Central in less than three months."

"Yeah, but the ones I'm interested in are the girls."

"Right. Because they're Sultan's girls and you're working for him."

"I didn't say that."

"You didn't have to. Anyway, I don't think you can overlook young Felix. It might all be connected."

"I don't see how, but, okay, go ahead."

"So, Felix's body is found after somebody is woke up by the noise. Amazing anybody at the Conquistador would bother to check, don't you think?"

"They must be slipping."

"Somebody took it to young Felix pretty good. His face was all caved in, and both arms were broken, and they'd carved on him some with a knife. Cut off his dick and his balls and carefully threw them in the trash can."

That made me squirm on the hard chair. Romero leaned toward me.

"And that's not the sick part."

"There's more?"

"Coroner found semen in the big gash where the guy's dick was supposed to be."

"You mean—"

"Someone made Felix into a girl and fucked him."

"Ah, Jesus—"

"Hey, it was what he always wanted. You didn't know Felix? He was a drag queen, a little beautician who worked weekends in high heels and tight dresses. He liked to surprise the johns with the fact he was a boy. He'd been in the hospital once or twice after johns busted him up, but he kept doing it. He needed the money."

"Drug habit?"

"Naw, Felix was clean. For his operation. Felix really wanted to be a girl, see, and he was saving up his blow-job money."

I was silent for a moment. "So he got his wish."

"Yeah, he was just too dead to know it."

"What makes you think all this is related to Sultan's girls?"

"The semen. Two of the hookers were raped. The coroner got the blood type from the semen and it appears to be the same."

"Could be coincidence."

"Sure could. But, hey, you wanted all the facts. There's Felix's story. You figure out how it fits. All I know is, it counts when the mayor's office calls down here and screams at us about four murders on the Cruise in less than three months."

I nodded. It must've been rough for Romero. His boss, a ruddy old-timer named Morgan, had retired recently, and the new Homicide chief was a dickhead named LeRoy Schulte whose best qualification is that he looks good in a suit. If the mayor's office was pouring heat on the department, Schulte doubtlessly funneled it to Romero. The election-time publicity generated by the Bible-thumpers couldn't be helping.

"Okay," he said, "so the second murder happened sometime the morning of April sixth. One of Sultan's girls, name of Hazel Melton, went by the name Busty. Anglo girl, thirty-two years old, already getting old for the Cruise, and her big tits were beginning to sag.

"She'd been beaten up pretty good, like she'd tried to fight and lost. Broken ribs, broken jawbone. Cut her, too. One of her tits was missing."

"Missing? Like not in the room?"

"Like not anywhere. We don't know where it went. Believe me, we've looked."

"Christ, this fucker's sick."

"If it's the same guy."

"But you said—"

"And you said the blood type could be a coincidence. That's the case. Now shut up and listen."

I nodded, pen poised, mouth shut.

"Third victim was the girl you found, Deena Meyers. I don't suppose you need to hear about her."

I shook my head, swallowed. I'd seen plenty of Deena.

"She was the only one who wasn't raped."

"But she was already dead. What, he wasn't in the mood?"

"Dead or alive doesn't seem to mean much to this dude when he's horny. If it's the same guy. I imagine he heard you coming before he could finish his business, and left by the window."

It had been that close. The guy must've still been in the room when Bongo heard the wailing, must've still been working on her. We'd just missed him.

"Fourth victim was done about four days ago," Romero continued. "Mulatto female went by Angelica. We still don't know her real name. Her prints weren't on file anywhere, so I guess she was new to the Cruise. The boys in Vice never heard of her.

"I say *about* four days ago because the coroner had trouble pinning it down. Her body was found day before yesterday after her landlord wondered about the smell coming from her room. She was busted up pretty good. Broken collarbone, right arm, skull fractures, the works."

"Not cut up?"

"No, looks like our boy started leaving his knife at home."

"If it's the same guy."

"Right. Look at the M.O.'s. They don't match up. He uses a knife, he doesn't use a knife. He beats them to a pulp, Deena hardly had a mark on her. One's a boy, the rest are girls. Go figure."

Exactly what I intended to do. I had to figure out the connection the police had missed if I was going to solve this before Felicia could.

"They all have one thing in common," Romero

said, reading my face. "No sign of forced entry. 'Course, with hookers, getting into the room is rarely the problem."

The gruesome descriptions hadn't made my stomach feel any better, but I managed to stand and thank Romero. He made a show of running me off as another detective arrived for work.

The burrito's aroma hadn't penetrated the elevator shaft, and my stomach steadied as the car hummed downstairs. I turned in my visitor's badge, stepped out into the still-cool morning air and headed back toward my car. Before I reached the corner of the building, someone shouted behind me.

I glanced over my shoulder—you never know what kind of crazies are hanging out around the cop shop—and saw two guys heading in my direction. The burly one had his hand raised, trying to get my attention. I recognized them, but acted like I didn't and hurried my steps.

"Mabry!" I froze, waited for them to catch up.

The burly plainclothes cop was Sergeant Kevin Borkum, a mean-spirited toad of a man with a crooked mustache running along his wide upper lip and an eye that floated off to one side so you could never tell where he was looking. The other was his partner, Officer Bates, a thin guy with a stoop, like his crew cut was too heavy for his skinny neck to hold up. Everybody calls him Norman behind his back.

Borkum and Bates have been working Vice together along the Cruise for six or seven years, long enough to see many sick things, and it's had its effect. They have that perverse us-against-the-world zeal that comes from being too tired too long. They wear matching black windbreakers and the same brand of sneakers and the same sneer. Doesn't matter they're too obvious for undercover. Every hooker in town knows their faces anyway.

I waited near some tall shrubs while Borkum waddled up to face me and Bates circled behind me like an emaciated ghost. Borkum stood too close, so I could smell his cigarette breath, and looked up into my face from the red-rimmed pouches that enclosed both eyes. I tried not to stare at the floater.

"You're Bubba Mabry, right?"

There was no denying it. Our paths had crossed before.

"What were you doing seeing Romero?"

"What do you mean? I was checking on a client."

Borkum stabbed my chest with a thick finger. "Don't bullshit me. I saw your name on the register. It said you were going to see Romero."

"Oh, well, yeah. That's true. Steve Romero is an old friend of mine and—"

He jabbed me again. I bristled, but I held my hands close to my sides and didn't move. Bates was close behind me.

"What *Lieutenant* Romero and I discuss is probably none of your business, Sergeant. If you want to know about it, ask him."

"I'm asking *you,* you fuck."

"Now, Sergeant, don't get rude." My mouth was running under its own power. The things that came out made me wince, but there was nothing I could do. When cornered, most people fight or fly or cower. I talk. "And tell Norman to stop breathing down my neck."

Bates muttered threateningly behind me, and I braced for the expected blow, but Borkum said, "This one's mine, Bates," and grabbed a handful of my shirt.

"Let go."

He pushed me backward, slammed me against the rough stucco wall, knocking the breath out of me. He pinned me there with his fist like a butterfly under glass. We were between the shrubs, invisible to the street.

Through gritted teeth I said, "Get your hands off me, you freak."

Borkum rocked back, but didn't let go of my shirt, so when he came forward again, his fist drove my sternum to the wall. It hurt. I coughed and sputtered, still nailed in place.

"Sultan Sweeney was seen at your place yesterday," he said, his breath hot on my face. "You working for him, you fuck?"

I said nothing. Bates danced around behind his partner, waiting for a chance to get at me.

"Don't deny it, shitheel." Borkum didn't need answers now. He had a full head of steam. "We know that's what you're doing. And now you've come by here to get Romero to help you out. Right?"

My voice came out raspy. "Something like that."

He tightened his grip on my shirt, pulled me closer. His knee slipped between my legs and pressed against my balls.

"Let me put this to you straight. Drop it. Right now. We don't want you dicking around in our business. Our turf, our collar. Understand?"

I couldn't just nod and get away. I had to say, "You know who did it?"

Borkum gave a little push with his knee, just enough to send a stab of pain upward through my belly.

"Just drop the fucking case."

My eyes were starting to water from the pressure on my balls. "Whatever you say," I squeaked.

Borkum's froggy mouth spread even wider. "Attaboy."

The pressure disappeared from between my legs and I sighed with relief and Borkum gave me one last push into the wall. It felt like the stucco pattern was permanently impressed in my back.

Borkum wiped his hands against each other, like I was something nasty he'd been forced to touch. Bates looked disappointed that he didn't get a crack at me.

As Borkum sauntered away, Bates paused long enough to say, "Next time, buddy boy. You fuck up, and you're mine next time."

My mouth opened but I snapped it shut before an insult escaped. He leered at me, waiting, then swaggered off after his partner. They'd managed to rough somebody up before breakfast. It was going to be a good day for Borkum and Bates.

6

I got back to my car, my chest aching, to find a parking ticket fluttering under the windshield wiper. The meter maids were working early. If Borkum and Bates hadn't held me up, I would've made it back before my quarter gave out. I snatched the ticket off the windshield and climbed behind the steering wheel and sat there for a moment, catching my breath.

Borkum's fist had left a sunburst of wrinkles on my shirtfront, and I smoothed them with my hand and tucked my shirttail tighter into my jeans. I unbuttoned the top few buttons and peeked in at my chest. It was an angry red, but it wouldn't bruise. Borkum knew what he was doing.

I buttoned up and drove away before the meter maid could circle by again. I'd had enough of the law for one day.

I swung over to Central Avenue and headed east, not really sure of my next move. The morning traffic was thick Downtown. Red lights stopped me between Broadway and Interstate 25, and I watched a spandexed hooker slip out of a pickup truck down the block, looking weary from a full night of working sex.

Tucked into this little three-block strip of cheap motels was one of the three hooker zones along Central that make up the Cruise. These girls mostly plied their trade with people drifting off the freeway. The one striding away up ahead looked like she might've taken on a whole carload of tourists. Her hair was disheveled and her shoulders stooped and she walked with her legs wide, like they wouldn't go back together anymore. I thought about stopping her, asking some questions, but I hesitated and she disappeared around a corner.

I hadn't recognized her, and it reminded me of how detached I'd grown from the action along the Cruise.

Years ago, I'd known everything about the Cruise and everybody along it, which hookers worked for which pimps, and who was in trouble and who gave away freebies. It was an easy, sleazy world of glowing neon and exhaust fumes and sloe-eyed women. There were dark pockets, sure. People who disappeared. Drug overdoses. The occasional body in a pool of blood. But overall there was a sense of gaiety, a street carnival of carnality.

Sex was different then. Everybody was doing it with wild abandon. Some were just getting paid for it. And what else could they do that would pay so well? Economically, prostitution was a good move for most of them, though it shortened their life spans and dropped many into the dark well of drugs they needed to face the everyday reality of it.

The victimless crime. Or at least that's what the newspapers called it. I'd seen it that way, too, I guess. How can it be a crime when the perpetrator is also the victim? The only person victimized in your typical quick roll is the hooker. Her life is the one that's cheapened. Prostitution is an escape valve for society, folks said. Take it away, and there'd be more rapes, more sex crimes. In everyday life, women control sex.

Buying a prostitute is the only time a man gets to dictate when and who and how.

There was talk of decriminalization. The laws weren't working anyway, people said, you can't legislate morality. A law can't prevent self-destruction. People are too bent on it.

Even the cops had adopted that attitude, too busy pursuing drug gangs and imagined terrorists to worry about a little nookie-for-hire. It was a freewheeling time along the Cruise.

Then AIDS came to town. It took a while for people to believe it. But once we watched a few people dry up and die terrible deaths, a gritty grimness settled over the Cruise. A few got out of the business, but most were in too deep. Or it was already too late. The virus might not develop into anything for years, but they already carried around a death sentence.

The public began putting pressure on the police, using the modern-day plague as their rallying cry. The city responded by unleashing bad dogs like Borkum and Bates on Central Avenue. There were more arrests, more deaths, more reason than ever for women to stay out of prostitution. Yet they kept popping up along the Cruise, drawn by money and whatever twisted mockery of self-esteem they got from being a rented receptacle for strangers' sperm.

Remembering the changes made me think where next to turn, and I bullied my way into the left-turn lane and drove onto the freeway. I swung onto I-40 at the huge crossroads everybody calls the "Big I," then drove west across the Rio Grande. Up onto Coors Boulevard—yes, a major thoroughfare named after a beer—then south to the modest, well-fenced home of Belinda Melville.

Belinda had been known as the White Whale when she was a jolly madam working girls along the Cruise.

After AIDS dropped its bomb on Central Avenue, she realized she was sending people to their deaths and she got out of the business.

She'd married a recently retired cop who'd been a regular customer for years. It had been a big, tense ceremony attended by half the police force and an equal number of hookers, grifters, and all-around lowlifes. And me.

Belinda was a teary, joyful bride, and her husband, a gruff old bastard, got ripping drunk at the reception, and it was quite a scene. Uniformed cops dancing with painted whores, detectives and informers having a few quiet words over drinks, a tableful of drag queens dishing in one corner. I counted three fistfights in the parking lot, but nobody was arrested and most people left drunk and happy.

I hardly ever saw Belinda anymore, but I knew she still kept tabs on her girls, still the Mother Hen to the ones who were left. Better than I'd done. I'd drifted away, trying to ignore the desperation and fear that lurked along the sidewalks.

Belinda's carport was empty, but I rang the bell anyway and the door opened. She filled the doorway, still a great painted ship of a woman, wearing a billowy housedress covered with giant pink flowers.

"Bubba! What a surprise!"

Though it was still early, she was in full makeup and her long drugstore-blond hair was perfect. Soap and flowers wafted through the screen door.

"Hi, Belinda, is your, uh, husband home?"

"Nah, Ralph's fishing at Cochiti Lake. Ralph's almost always out fishing."

She followed my glance toward her empty carport and said, "My car's in the shop, so I'm stuck here until he gets home. Why don't you come on in?"

I glanced nervously at the quiet street, said a silent

prayer that Ralph had stumbled on to a school of bass, and slipped through the door.

Belinda's tastes in furnishings still leaned toward brocade wallpaper and brass chandeliers, and the inside of the house had a crowded opulence that belied its exterior. If you didn't look too close.

Belinda sat me in a worn red chair with lace doilies on the arms and fluttered around me like a moth, saying how good I looked and how long it had been. The housedress was snug around her ample breasts and her broad hips, but loose in the right places, and she still looked like someone you'd want to snuggle all night.

"I don't drink coffee anymore," she said, "but there's some iced tea. Want some?"

I said sure, and she sauntered to the kitchen, her big hips swinging. The size of her, her acres of fair skin, made me think of mounds of vanilla ice cream, enough to dive into. I felt a little tingle in my groin, and memories of gleefully sweaty nights with lusty fat women flashed through my mind.

I've always had a weakness for meaty women. They're softer and smoother and feel womanly in your hands. It had been a long time since I'd taken a tumble with a woman with some padding. Felicia's a nicely built little woman, understand, I'm not complaining. But something in me still longed for a mountain of moonlit flesh.

Belinda brought the tea and sat on the sofa near me in a flounce of perfume. She crossed her legs and her shins were red and splotchy. She saw me looking and self-consciously stroked one leg with her hand, testing its smoothness.

"Had my legs waxed yesterday, and they damn near tore all the hide off," she said. "It goes away in a day or two."

The thought of having my leg hairs ripped out by

the roots gave me the squeams. I tore my eyes away and changed the subject.

We talked about old times awhile and she updated me on her former employees. One had gone off to Arizona. One had married a truck driver and called it quits. Two had died, one downed by AIDS and one bludgeoned with a hammer a year earlier. A couple still worked the Cruise, against Belinda's advice.

"Any of them working for a pimp named Sultan Sweeney?"

"Lord, no, I'd take a girl in under my own roof before I'd let her work for that snake."

"I take it you know Sultan."

"I know of him. Enough to know I wouldn't let my girls get near him. Don't you read the papers? Three of his girls have been killed. That's not good business."

"He feels the same way."

"You know him?"

"I'm working for him. He hired me to investigate the deaths."

"Get outta here."

"I'm serious."

"Oh, shit, honey, you should know better. Sultan Sweeney is a bad man. He's cut up a few of his girls in the past. Girls who were holding out on him, or not performing to his standards. One look at the little sonuvabitch ought to tell a girl he's bad news. But they follow him around like baby ducks, in *love* with him. Love and business don't mix, Bubba."

"Tell me."

"So how come you're working for Sultan?"

"Well, it's a long story, but I figure it like this: Somebody needs to catch whoever's killing those girls, and it might as well be me. If Sultan's the one who pays the tab, all the better. Maybe his girls get some good out of him after all."

She looked skeptical, took a slug of tea while she thought it over, set the glass down on the dusty coffee table.

"So that's why you're here today? To see if I know anything about the murders?"

"I thought you might've heard something through your girls, talk on the street. I've been sort of out of touch."

"Nah, I don't know anything about it, Bubba. I haven't talked to any of the girls in the past couple of weeks. As long as it's just Sultan's girls who are getting it, they probably think there's no sense worrying me."

"It's not just Sultan's girls. The cops think the same person might've done a drag queen who was killed back in March. Some guy named Felix?"

I could tell by her expression that she'd heard about Felix.

"Well, that changes things," she said. "If it's just Sultan's girls, then I'd say it was Sultan who was killing them."

"I thought about that. But then why would he hire me?"

Belinda tried to fight back a smile. "Maybe that's why, Bubba. Maybe it's a smoke screen. You've talked to the cops?"

"Uh-huh."

"And you told them you're working for Sultan?"

"Not exactly, but I think they figured it out."

She let the smile spread wide. "Don't you think that's what Sultan wanted to happen? Maybe he thinks hiring a private eye will show the cops he's as interested in solving the murders as they are."

That hadn't occurred to me, and it took me a minute to swallow it.

"But why take the risk? I mean, if he did it. Doesn't he have to worry about me finding him out?"

Belinda pursed her lips, trying to think of the right way to say it.

"Maybe he doesn't know you the way the rest of us do. I mean, maybe he thinks you'll be easy to fool or something. There was all that business in the papers about Elvis Presley. . . ."

I choked on my tea and coughed and hacked until I could breathe again. Belinda talked the whole time.

"I'm sorry, Bubba. I didn't mean to upset you. That's probably not it at all. I mean, you have a sterling reputation down on the Cruise. If he asked anybody about you, they'd tell him—"

I waved her off, and managed to say between gasps, "That's okay, Belinda. Don't worry about it."

"I really am sorry, Bubba."

"No, no, it's fine. My tea just went down the wrong pipe."

There was an uncomfortable silence while Belinda tried to think of something else comforting to say.

"Let's say Sultan really doesn't have anything to do with the murders," I said. "Who do you think could've done it?"

"Oh, Bubba, it could've been anybody. That's the thing about the Cruise. So many people passing through, so much happening so fast. There's no way to really keep up with it. All those killings could've been coincidental. You know what I mean? Different killers, different reasons. It happens all the time on the Cruise, girls getting killed. It's just been oftener lately."

I was getting frustrated. "Let's say the same guy did them all. Then what've you got?"

"That doesn't narrow it down much, Bubba. You know we get all kinds down there. Bikers, married men, boys getting their first poke, people passing through. It could be one of those crazy drifters like

71

you read about in the papers all the time. Someone who gets a kick out of killing people."

Oh, please, don't let it be a drifter. How would I ever track him down? He'd probably be long gone by now, blown off down the freeway like a deadly tumbleweed. Of course, then Felicia wouldn't be able to find him either. . . .

"I tell you what it could be," Belinda continued. "It could be one of those holy rollers who've been making all the noise. Some of them are pretty crazy. Maybe one decided to take matters into his own hands."

Reverend Skip Jericho flashed through my mind, wiping his forehead with his handkerchief. I remembered the way those Christian youths had hustled away the drunk at the rally.

Still, I said, "I don't know, Belinda . . ."

"Then your guess is as good as mine," she said, a little shortly. She'd been willing to brainstorm with me, but I hadn't been able to generate so much as a raindrop of my own, and she'd grown tired of my naysaying.

"Well, listen, Belinda, I appreciate you taking the time to talk to me. I wish I'd come under more pleasant circumstances."

She rose with me and trailed me to the door.

"That's okay, Bubba. It's always good to see anybody from the old crowd. Sometimes, I feel like I'm trapped out here in the suburbs, missing all the fun."

"It's not much fun anymore."

That sobered her. "I know, Bubba. I know."

She reached out to pat me, ended up giving me a cushy hug. She looked like her eyes might tear up as she broke the clinch.

"You know, Bubba, there is someone else you might ask. There's this woman, Rosie Corona, who's started that group SCORE?"

"I've heard about her."

"She knows everybody. Maybe she'd be willing to help."

Belinda gave me an address in the North Valley, another hug, and waved good-bye from the door as I walked to my car.

"Good luck. I hope you find whoever's doing it."

I shouted my thanks and waved over the roof of the car. As I ducked inside, I heard her call one more thing: "My money's still on Sultan Sweeney."

Fourth Street, north of Downtown, is much like Central Avenue, an old commercial strip left to its own devices after being bypassed by the freeways thirty years ago. Dotted with cheap kitchenettes and failing shops and empty diners.

Central had made something of a comeback, with little zones of trendy bistros and bookstores springing up to draw pedestrians, and the attractions of the Cruise to keep cars filling the street. North Fourth hadn't been so lucky. The traffic patterns kept shifting ever farther away, and storefronts were boarded up and the supermarkets were converted into bingo halls.

Because of the rural pretensions of the North Valley, with its horses and alfalfa fields, North Fourth had a different character—pickup trucks and feed stores, potholes and firewood yards. Old houses that clung to the shoulders of the four-lane had been converted into antique shops and septic tank repair places and beauty salons, looking ever more ragged with each change of ownership.

As I drove out North Fourth toward the address

Belinda had given me, I spotted a sign outside a swaybacked old farmhouse that caused me to stop and turn around. Loopy letters on a pink background said DELBERT'S DOLLS.

I'd seen the place listed in the yellow pages and had been meaning to check it out for my other case, the one I'd barely thought about for two days. I whipped into the empty gravel parking lot.

A bell jangled as I swung open the door. Bright sunlight gave way to fluorescent-punctuated dimness, and my eyes took a second to adjust. What I saw made me step back.

Dolls stared down at me from every direction. Shelves and shelves of them, floor to rafters. Baby dolls and porcelain belles and Barbies. Round-headed waifs and cheerleaders and gnomes. A zoo's worth of plush animals—whales and hippos, giraffes and elephants, lions and tigers and bears, oh my. Hundreds were packed tightly on the shelves, right up to the edge, like a crowd on a subway platform. They all stared with unblinking eyes, all turned just right to be looking at you when you walked in the door.

"Can I help you?"

The high-pitched voice rose from somewhere in the shadowy recesses at the back of the room. I shielded my eyes from the fluorescent tubes and peered back there. I saw no one.

"Over here."

I took a step forward, the dolls watching carefully. Everyone I could see looked like they'd need somebody to pull their chains before they could talk.

A little man popped up from behind a glass-front counter like a jack-in-the-box. I jumped.

"Hi. Sorry. I was on my knees unpacking some boxes."

Even up off his knees, the little man wasn't much

taller than the counter. I narrowed my eyes at him, but he blinked like he hadn't spooked me on purpose, and I let it go.

He had a disappearing chin, sloping shoulders, and a layer of baby fat accentuated by stretched red suspenders. His bald head was shiny pink, and he wore tiny, wire-rimmed glasses that fit tight against his brows. His voice was a high-pitched whine just this side of effeminate. All in all, he looked and sounded like he should be on a shelf with a price tag on his toe.

"You must be Delbert."

"That's me. What can I do for you today?"

"My name is Bubba Mabry and I'm a private investigator." I gave him one of my cards and he looked it over, frowning. "I'm investigating the theft of some dolls, and I was wondering whether anybody might've tried to sell them to you."

"A theft? Here in Albuquerque?" He looked alarmed.

"Yeah, about a week ago."

"A whole collection?"

"Yeah."

"Oh, my. Whose was it?"

"I'm afraid I can't say. You've probably never heard of it anyway. It hasn't been displayed anywhere."

"Hmmm."

I'd put the Polaroids of the dolls in my shirt pocket before I got out of the car, and the photos' sharp corners caught in there as I tried to fish them out. I wedged them this way and that, trying to get them loose.

"This is quite a place you've got here."

"Thank you. Biggest selection in town. You're welcome to look around if you want."

I finally freed the photos and handed them over. He

looked at each one, hmming and aahing like he
appreciated what he saw.

I rocked on my heels and looked around. We were in
what once had been the living room of the old house,
and I could see through a doorway other rooms
packed just as full with dolls and toys. I had a brief
horror movie fantasy of being trapped in there, all the
dolls staring while I waited for the first one to move.
Killer Babes in Toyland, something like that.

"These are excellent!" Delbert declared when he'd
finished sorting through the photos.

"Yeah?"

"Oh, my, yes. They're some of the best I've seen.
Very old, but still in great condition. I'd like to see the
real things."

"I would, too. So would the person who owns
them."

"I would really like to meet the collector," Delbert
said. "I love to chat with someone who knows their
dolls."

"Well, I'll mention that to my client. Maybe she'll
give you a call. But I doubt it."

"Too bad." He shrugged and flapped his pudgy
hands.

"So I take it nobody's brought these dolls around,
trying to sell them."

"No. And I'd remember dolls like those."

"They're pretty valuable, huh?"

He looked me over with a sharp eye. "I hardly think
your client would've hired you otherwise."

Now it was my turn to shrug. "Afraid I don't know
much about dolls."

"Well, kewpies aren't my forte, either," Delbert
said. "That's why I don't have any in the shop. But
some collectors are crazy about them. All part of the
folk art fad."

He said it with some disdain, and I knew better than to pursue it.

"Are they rare?"

"Fairly so, yes, at least high-quality ones like these. The old ones are well-detailed, but they're delicate, so there aren't that many left."

"Delicate, huh?"

"Oh, yes. Some have heads of a type of cheap porcelain they used before plastic came along. Plus, they have feathers and tiny legs that must be handled with care. They weren't meant to last forever. They were just carnival prizes, usually long gone by the next time the carnival came to town."

"Would there be much of a market for stolen ones?"

Delbert put a hand to his plump chin and thought it over.

"If the thief knew a collector, or was a collector himself, then yes, of course. But if it's just some burglar, it's unlikely he'll know what he has. Even if he did, collectors are difficult to locate. He couldn't very well take out a booth at the annual doll show."

Which brought me back to my original theory: that neighborhood kids had lifted the dolls and probably were playing with the fragile valuables in the mud somewhere right now. The doll collection, some jewelry, and a few other small items were all that had been taken. Kids.

I thanked him and backed away toward the door. All the dolls and teddy bears still seemed to stare at me, following me with their eyes.

"How do you do that anyway?"

"Do what?"

My cheeks warmed, and I couldn't believe what I was saying.

"How do you turn those dolls so it looks like they're all looking down at the customers?"

Delbert smiled primly. "I assure you, Mr. Mabry,

they're up there haphazardly. Customers rifle through them all the time. Does it feel like they're staring at you?"

"No, no. Well, yeah."

He chuckled, touched a finger to his lips to shush himself.

"Maybe it's just their little souls peering out," he said.

I ran a hand over my face and shook my head.

"It's been a long day already, and it's not even lunchtime."

He nodded and chuckled some more.

"I'll call you if anybody drops by with these dolls, but it isn't very likely."

"I know."

"Good day."

Out in the dusty parking lot, I took a deep breath and gazed up at the high blue New Mexico sky and the claustrophobia eased its grip. The daily wind was just starting to breeze into town, and I felt the sweat on my forehead cool and dry. I climbed into the Chevy and rattled out onto North Fourth.

A coffee shop snuggled among some cottonwoods up ahead on the left, and I steered into the parking lot. I needed a break . . . some coffee to clear my head. Working two cases at once left me feeling distracted, jumbled. Of course, the problem didn't come up too often. Usually I was lucky to have one case.

The café was one of those franchise joints whose trademark is a toaster on every table. I never have understood that concept. Why don't they just bring you some freaking toast? Are there people who are so concerned with getting their toast just right that they want to do it themselves? Toast connoisseurs?

One time, I ate at a steakhouse in El Paso, Texas, where the grills sat right out in the middle of the room and the raw meat was displayed in glass-front coolers.

You picked out your steak like it was a lobster, and then you could stand over the cook while he grilled it. Or they'd hand you the spatula and you could grill it yourself. All these potbellied barbecue nuts standing around with forks in their hands, talking the manly art of cooking outdoors. Me, I kept thinking about health codes and colon cancer and flying spit.

The coffee shop menu went on for pages and pages, but I couldn't focus on it. A middle-aged waitress with a pile of brunette hair lacquered on top of her head appeared at my table, pen poised, gum popping.

"What can I get you?" She spoke out the side of her mouth, which was a red slash across her powdered face, never missing a beat on that gum.

"Burger and fries. Coffee. No toast."

She pulled up on her gum-chewing for half a second, cut her eyes over to me for a hard look and said, "Uh-*huh*." Then she snapped her pad shut and disappeared.

I tried not to think about finding chewed gum in my food. I was fiddling with the knobs on the toaster when the waitress silently appeared again to give me a disapproving look. I thought she set the coffee cup down a little hard, but I didn't say anything, just smiled and nodded.

I don't know what it is about me that sets people off. Been that way all my life, especially with authority figures. In school, I was always the one the teachers caught. Something about the way I stood with my shoulders slumped, a certain hangdog quality about my face, something about me looked guilty.

And then there's my mouth, which sometimes takes on a life of its own, blurting out the one thing that will get me in the most trouble. Like that business with the dolls. I couldn't just keep my mouth shut and race out of there. I had to rant about how they were looking at me. Delbert probably thought I was crazy, probably tossed my card in the trash.

I heard myself sigh just as the waitress popped up again, but her features didn't soften at the sound. She turned away before I could ask for some ketchup.

An old guy at the next table teetered to his feet and ambled toward the cash register. He'd left his newspaper folded neatly, but he didn't look like he was coming back for it. I reached across and snatched it and spread it out beside my plate. If I was going to sit and eat dry fries until my nerves stopped jangling, I might as well catch up with whatever Felicia was doing.

Sure enough, there she was on the front page with a story about the rally. The righteous black-and-white images of Reverend Skip Jericho and the Dudleys stared up at me, their mouths open in song. Her story was a thorough, accurate account, though there was no mention of the disturbance by the drunk. I thought that had been the best part of the rally, but Felicia's editors probably wouldn't let her include it.

It was a comfort to see she'd done a good job. You want the person you love to be good at what they do. You want to be proud of them. I tried not to dwell on Felicia's opinions about what I do for a living.

Of course, since I'd been at the rally, I didn't learn anything from the story that might help me solve the murders. But it occurred to me I'd be able to track most everything Felicia could come up with, just by reading the newspaper. That gave me an advantage in our little race. I carefully tore out the story and stuffed it in my pocket to be filed later.

I leafed through the rest of the paper while I ate my lunch. Not much else that interested me, just the same old revolutions and famines and catastrophes. One item grabbed my eye, though. Deep inside the paper was a full page of photos and profiles of the people running for City Council in Tuesday's primary election, Republicans on the top half of the page and Democrats across the bottom. I scanned across, looking for the faces I knew.

Quentin Dudley looked serious in his photo, his wide jaw clenched and his brow furrowed in concern for his constituents. The brief profile said he was a forty-year-old lawyer who'd represented his Northeast Heights district for four years and who was proudest of his work campaigning against crime.

His opponent in the Republican primary was a thick-mustached Spanish fellow name of Stan Gutierrez. It was his first run at the council, but he had a dazzling smile and a decent résumé and the right last name. Lot of people out here still vote a straight ticket along ethnic lines. But the Northeast Heights isn't exactly teeming with Hispanics, and it was my bet Gutierrez didn't have a prayer whipping somebody as visible as Dudley. After all, who had his picture on the front page?

The Democratic candidate running for Dudley's seat was unopposed in the primary, but they still ran his photo and profile, just to be equitable. He was a gray-haired old pol named Stoney Davis, who'd held nearly every other job in city government over the past thirty years. Guess he decided it was time to step up to the council and be the boss awhile. If I lived in his district, I thought, I'd pull this guy's lever in the voting booth. Better to have an old fixer who knows how things work than some do-gooder like Dudley.

While I was downpage among the Democrats, I checked out the profile on Alice Burden. She, too, was unopposed, and she beamed in her photo, peeking out from under the brim of one of her large, lavish hats. You had to look close to see the toughness in her eyes, a glint that said, Damned right, I'm unopposed, who'd dare come after me?

Alice Burden has a build like Bella Abzug and a voice like Ethel Merman and the political cunning of Lyndon B. Johnson. She wears wide-brimmed hats with bouquets and waxed fruit on them, and I think she knows Liberace's tailor. She's loud and brassy and she knows how to draw a crowd. The rest of the City Council is scared to death of her.

But I knew Alice Burden had a soft spot. Somewhere in there, under the hats and the brass and the clouds of Chanel No. 5, beat the heart of a sentimental woman. And someone had stolen that woman's doll collection.

Alice Burden had called me a week earlier and invited me to her home to discuss a case. She lived alone in a neat little ivy-covered cottage near the university, where she taught classes when she wasn't stirring up trouble at City Hall. I'd put on a sport coat for the occasion, which is pretty dressy for me. I refuse to wear neckties.

Alice met me in her living room with a silver tray, and over coffee told me about her burglary. Ten five-inch-tall kewpie dolls had been arranged in a blue-velvet-lined box on top of an upright piano. Even a stupid burglar would've seen they were worth something, displayed like that. And a kid would've gone nuts for them.

"So," I said when she finished, "these dolls are valuable?"

"Well, they were expensive," she brayed. "But their value involves more than money. If it was just the money, I'd take the insurance settlement and be living on my high hog."

Like most New Mexico politicians, Alice Burden never met a mixed metaphor she didn't like. Our governor once referred to someone "opening a box of Pandoras."

"But there's a certain sentimental value."

"How's that?"

She looked me over, deciding whether to tell. Then she said, "It's all confidential?"

"Absolutely."

Alice shifted on the sofa and sat forward, ready to dish. "When I was a young girl, I had a, um, romantic fling."

My eyebrows must've rose, because she laughed and slapped her knee.

"Hard to believe now, isn't it, Bubba? But this saggy old body used to have men swarming around like bees at a honey pot."

I laughed with her, and mumbled something polite.

"One summer I met this man who worked at the carnival. Oh, he was a rough old boy. He had tattoos and greasy blue jeans and my parents would've keeled over at the sight of him. But he was soft on the inside, gentle, and I was crazy about him."

"So what happened?"

"Well, the carnival left town, of course. And he went with it. I'd probably just been a pleasant diversion for him, but it seemed like more than that. When he left, he gave me one of those kewpie dolls as a parting gift."

She sorted through the Polaroids of her collection until she came up with the right doll, then passed it across to me. The doll was a little more tattered than the others, its pencil-thin eyebrows nearly gone and the red feathers that sprang from behind it limp. Alice Burden looked a little misty as she handed me the other photographs.

"I kept that doll a long time. Eventually, I collected the others so I could set it out in the open without raising too many questions. It gave me a warm feeling to see it over there."

I nodded understandingly and agreed to take the case.

Private eyes don't often get stolen goods cases. We can't do much more than the police, contacting pawnshops, getting the word out. And, while the police might not do much on the typical residential burglary, you can bet they'd pulled out the stops when it came to a city councilwoman's stolen dolls.

I took the case, I told myself, because of the sentimental angle. And I desperately needed the money to pay my taxes. Alice Burden seemed to understand such an investigation could be lengthy and expensive and might not produce any results. My specialty.

Besides, having a member of the City Council for a client had to be good for business, right?

8

Rosie Corona's house looked like a fortress, an old thick-walled adobe with small, crooked windows and pointed roof beams that bristled from the walls like spears. The mud-colored house squatted in the middle of a field under a couple of huge cottonwood trees, all surrounded by a chain-link fence.

I parked in the dusty driveway outside the gate, tooted the horn, and stepped out of the car. I'm six feet tall, and the fence must've been eight because I could've just about reached the top.

The screen door opened and a black bolt of lightning shot from it, racing toward me.

Rahr-rahr-rahr-rar-rar!

The damned Doberman didn't make a sound until it scrabbled to a stop at the fence. Then it roared at me through chopping fangs, bouncing around behind the fence, froth dripping from its jaws. Startled, I stumbled backward and sat down hard in the dust.

"Baby!"

The barking died in mid-*rahr*. Baby's butt dropped to the ground and he sat quivering, licking his chops, watching me.

A dark-haired woman stood in the doorway of the house. She wore cutoff jeans and a loose shirt tied at her waist Daisy Mae style. She was barefoot.

"Get up off your ass and tell me what you want," she shouted over the wind. A fine greeting.

I scrambled to my feet and brushed at the back of my jeans.

"Hi, uh, I'm Bubba Mabry. I'm a private investigator and I'm looking into some murders. I'd like to talk to you about them."

"Why?"

"Why?"

"Yeah. Why me? I don't know nothing about any murders."

"Oh, right. Well, I thought you could give me some information about people on the Cruise."

She looked me over. She was petite and well tended, and she looked tropical in her summer clothes.

"All right," she said. "Come on in."

I cast nervous glances at the dog, and Rosie Corona said, "Baby'll sit right there unless I tell him to do otherwise."

"Okay, if you say so."

Sometimes you have to show people you trust them. It's the only way to get them to trust you. If she said the big dog would stay put, then I'd just have to trust that she knew what she was talking about. I slipped open the gate, took a deep breath, and stepped inside the fence.

God, I hate dogs. In my line of work, most of the dogs you see are like this one: heat-seeking chain saws trained to rip open trespassers. There's no reasoning with them, no bullshitting your way out of a situation. It's primal, and it gives me chills.

Baby sat perfectly still, except for his butt, which twitched with excitement. The muscles rippled under his black skin. I edged past him toward the low porch, then watched over my shoulder as I picked my way up the steps and into the house.

As soon as the screen door slammed shut, Baby jumped up and trotted to the door. Then he sat down in front of it and watched us through the screen, a silent sentinel. I imagined one wrong move would send the dog ripping through the screen and bounding toward my throat. I sat very carefully in the chair Rosie indicated, but I kept glancing back over my shoulder at Baby.

"Relax," Rosie said. "Baby is perfectly trained. He won't do anything unless I tell him. He just likes to keep an eye on things."

I wondered briefly whether Rosie Corona still received johns here in her little fort of a home. Imagine trying to get it up while this panting beast watched from the doorway. But how could she still be in the business when she'd gone public with SCORE? The cops probably watched her all the time.

Boxes of SCORE pamphlets filled one corner of the living room, and pamphlets and envelopes and a mailing list all were piled on the coffee table, alongside an overflowing ashtray. Not the most romantic setting. The rest of the house looked plain, underdecorated, like it had been burgled often.

The covers of the pamphlets said, in big letters, SLAVES NO MORE, YOU CAN SCORE. I picked one up and opened it. Inside was a photograph of a woman at a typewriter. I thought she wore just a little too much makeup for secretarial work. The other picture showed a weary, smiling mom rocking her daughter in her lap.

"So what can I do for you?"

I dropped the pamphlet on the coffee table and looked up at her. She leaned toward me, her elbows on her knees, and I could see down her shirt, and she saw me looking and didn't blink. Her face was all business and her dark eyes were hard.

"I was sent here by an old friend of mine, Belinda Melville?"

She nodded just enough to show she knew Belinda.

"Belinda and I are sort of out of touch with things along the Cruise, but she said you know everybody."

"I know a lot of people." She sat back coolly, crossed her legs. She'd plucked a burning cigarette from the ashtray, and she took a drag and the smoke filled a shaft of sunlight that fell between us from the front door. The dog's long shadow lay on the floor to my right, and I kept seeing it out of the corner of my eye and jerking my head around.

"So," I said, turning back to her nervously, "I'm looking into the four murders of prostitutes along Central, or, uh, more specifically, of the three women—"

The cops could solve Felix's murder on their own.

"—and I thought you might have some ideas about people I could talk to. Or maybe you have some theories about who did it."

"Why would I have theories? That's a job for the police. I'm too busy with SCORE to sit around worrying over the newspapers."

I hadn't said anything about newspapers, so I knew she'd been keeping up with the investigation.

"Come on, Miss Corona, play detective with me. If you were looking into this, where would you start?"

She didn't smile, but her face softened a little, like she was thinking, What could it hurt?

"All right, Mr. . . . . Mabry, is it?"

"Call me Bubba."

"All right, Bubba. I'll play along. For a minute anyway."

"Great. So where would you start?"

"Well, I suppose I'd begin by thinking about what

the three women have in common. Or what the murders have in common."

"They all happened in motel rooms," I said. "The women were all prostitutes. They, uh, all look like they were done by a strong man."

Through the smoke I could see a scowl take over her face, like she was impatient with me already. I clammed up.

"Those could all be coincidences," she said witheringly. "The one thing they had in common is they worked for Sultan Sweeney."

"Yeah? So?"

"So shouldn't you start with him?"

"Oh. Well, this all sort of began with him. . . ."

"What do you mean?" Something about the way her voice went cold told me I'd better be careful.

"Just, uh, that I talked to him first. A little, anyway. He didn't say much."

"He wouldn't. He has too much to lose."

"You think he did those girls?"

"What do *you* think?"

She'd exhaled another cloud of smoke, and it glowed in the sunlight. I squinted, trying to read her obscured face. I didn't want to say the wrong thing, but I wasn't sure which way to jump. Baby growled somewhere behind me.

"Well, I don't rightly know. . . ."

Rosie Corona said nothing for a long time. She leaned forward, stubbed out her cigarette in the ashtray. Then she sat back, sort of twisted on the couch like she was getting comfortable. Her hand came up from between the cushions with a flat black automatic, and she pointed it at me as casually as you'd point your finger.

"You're working for him, aren't you?"

I swallowed hard and said, "How's that?"

"You're working for Sultan Sweeney."

"Me? Naw, I—"

"Don't lie to me."

"Yes, ma'am, I am."

"You've got a lot of fucking nerve coming here."

"Now, Miss Corona, I don't know what this is all about. I'm unarmed and I don't think you—"

"Shut up."

"Look, this is all some kind of misunderstanding—"

She snapped the slide back on the pistol to slam a round into the chamber. I shut up.

"Sultan Sweeney's sent goons around before, but never one as inept as you."

I was too busy shaking to be insulted. There apparently was some powerful history between this woman and Sultan Sweeney, and I'd stumbled into it blindly. I didn't really think she'd shoot me, but I didn't know how to get out of it gracefully. I would have been happy to run for it, but Baby stood growling at the door.

Rosie Corona watched me sweat, like she was deciding what to do with me.

"How long have you been working for him?"

"For Sweeney? About twenty-four hours. He hired me yesterday afternoon."

I thought I saw a hint of a smile through the smoke and the shadows. It didn't make me feel any better.

"So he sent you directly to me?"

"He didn't send me. I told you. It was Belinda Melville."

"Sultan never mentioned me?"

"No, ma'am."

There was a pause.

"Then, mister, I'd say you had some bad luck."

I nodded somberly. This notion has plagued me for years. Sometimes I feel like the jinx in the Lil' Abner comics of my youth, the sad little guy with the black cloud over his head. Like in the cartoons, my bad luck often strikes those who get too close to me. Occasionally, like now, I take a direct hit.

She was silent, and it seemed time to plead my case, but I didn't know what to say. I couldn't read this woman. A trickle of sweat tickled its way down my ribs while the seconds ticked past. I swallowed and spoke, low and croaky as a deacon.

"I didn't mean any harm, ma'am."

She'd been holding the gun in the shaft of light while she sat in shadow, and it seemed to float there on its own accord, steady as a rock. Now the barrel wavered, drifted away, though it stayed pointed in my general direction.

Rosie Corona sighed.

"I don't want to kill anybody today. I've got too much to do."

"That would be fine by me."

"Get up and get out of here."

I eased to my feet, keeping my hands out away from my body, and edged toward the door. The barrel of the pistol tracked my every move.

A low growl from the porch froze me in place, and I said, "Ma'am? The dog . . ."

"Baby! Back off!"

The dog turned from the door and trotted off into the yard. I watched while he squatted in the dust between me and the gate.

"He'll be okay?"

"You just march on out of here and let me worry about Baby."

Rosie was on her feet now, the pistol still aimed at me, and I didn't stand around and argue.

I walked slowly down the steps, watching the dog. He looked from me to Rosie and back again and whined, like he sensed something was wrong. Maybe he understood what it meant when his owner kept a gun trained on somebody.

Hands still in the air, I stepped sideways to give the beast a wide berth. I was halfway to the fence when a rumble rose from Baby's throat and he broke from his obedient squat.

My feet took off on their own. The fence loomed up ahead, but it suddenly seemed an impossible distance away. No way I could outrun Baby. He had twice as many legs as me, and he was in better shape. But I ran, looking back over my shoulder at the snapping jaws closing in on me. My body reacted automatically, I guess, because all I can remember is Baby's face, that black-and-tan blur of saliva and snarl.

Rahr-rahr-rahr-rar-rar!

I hit the fence high, and the wires cut into my fingers as I pulled myself up. My feet scrabbled for purchase, too big to toe through the links.

Rosie Corona shouted, "Baby!"

Baby leaped behind me, and I felt a dull thud against my kidneys and his warm breath on my back. A ripping sound filled the air, and I thought it was my bones and I threw myself over the top of the fence.

It was a long way down. Fortunately, I landed on my butt. I fell back onto my elbows, and my head snapped back and the whole world seemed to whirl for a moment. When it stopped, I felt my bare back with one hand. Everything seemed intact.

Baby stood on the other side of the fence, munching away at a large piece of my blue shirt, giving it angry little shakes with his head.

Rosie Corona still stood on her porch, the gun dangling loose beside her. Her eyes looked a little wide.

"Are you all right?"

"I think so." I picked·myself up, feeling the creaks

and aches where I'd flattened on impact. I brushed the dust off my bloodied hands and cranked my head around to look at what was left of my shirt. The whole back was gone, from the shoulder blades down. Baby seemed to be polishing off the last of it, happily chewing away.

"You shouldn't have run," Rosie said. "It set him off."

"That's a dangerous dog." Now that I was alive, I was getting indignant.

"That's right," she said. "You tell that to Sultan Sweeney."

She turned and went inside. The screen door slammed shut.

9

I felt like I'd been ate by a bear and shit off a cliff. My ribs ached and my fingers stung and my back hurt and my left elbow was sprained enough for the throb to be steady. My head swam with dolls and cops and corpses and fangs.

Somehow, I made it home. By the time I calmed down, I was stretched in my armchair, a glass of Kentucky's finest in my hand and my ripped shirt lying across the bed where I could see it. It had been damned close. I suppressed a shudder, downed my drink, and moved to the bed. What I needed, for a little while anyway, was to sleep.

The sheets were cool against my bare back, and I made myself lie completely still and closed my eyes. Pretty soon the swirling images began to slow, and my breathing followed suit. I felt myself relaxing into the mattress.

Then the telephone rang. I snapped upright, setting off pangs that took my breath away.

"Hullo?"

"Bubba? Alice Burden here."

"Oh, hi. What's up?"

"Just the rent and the price of beans." She giggled sportingly when I didn't respond. "But seriously, Bubba, I was wondering how the case is going."

I thought: Me, too.

"Oh, it's going right along," I said. "I'm getting the word out to stores and things, which is always the first step."

"No leads yet, eh?"

"Not really."

"Okay, well, I know you'll give it your best stab. I sure miss my little dolls."

"Yes, ma'am, I'm sure you do. I'm doing everything I can, but I've also got this other case . . ."

"Oh? You work on several cases at a time?"

"Well, not several. Two. And this other one involves murder, so it's pretty rough going."

My back cracked to remind me just how rough.

"Murder? Really?"

"Yes, ma'am, the prostitute murders down here on Central Avenue. But don't worry. I'm only billing you for the time I actually spend hunting your dolls."

"Oh, I'm not worried about that, Bubba. I trust you completely."

I didn't know whether to be flattered or embarrassed. I reminded myself Alice Burden was a politician, and such things trip off their tongues with ease.

"I'll call you soon as I have anything."

"All right, Bubba. When you can. Sounds like this other case has got you burning your britches at both ends."

After I hung up, I creaked back down onto my elbows, then flat on the bed. I knew I should get up and wash off the dust, maybe let the shower run its hot fingers over my sore muscles. But all I wanted to do was sleep.

I was lying there with my eyes closed, thinking how

getting older was affecting my recuperative powers, when my telephone jangled again. I'd learned my lesson last time. I let the damned thing ring a few times while I crept across the bed and reached the receiver off the hook.

"Bubba. Where y'at?"

"What?"

"How you doin'? Sultan Sweeney callin'."

That made me sit up. "Yessir." My mouth tasted cottony. "What can I do for you?"

"What I wanta know is, what've you *been* doin' for me?"

His voice sounded tinny, like he was calling from a car phone or one of those pocket-sized portables.

"Oh, you want a progress report."

"If dat idn't too much to ask. I'm payin' you a lot of money. I figure I'm entitled to know what's happenin'."

"Sure, sure. No problem. I, uh, talked to the cops and to some people—"

"The cops? You say anythin' about me?"

"Of course not." Almost the truth.

"Awright. Go ahead."

"And I talked to some people who know the Cruise to see if they'd heard anything."

"Uh-huh."

I had to tread carefully now. "And I went to see Rosie Corona."

"Rosie Corona? What de hell she got to do with it?"

"Looks like nothing. Though she's not your biggest fan."

"You got dat right. Dat little bitch been givin' me a load of trouble. Couple my girls run off to be secretaries 'cause of her."

"Yeah, well, she figured out I was working for you and chased me out of her house with a gun. That damned dog of hers about ate my ass off."

I thought I heard Sultan chuckle.

"Dat is one big dog she's got."

"Fast, too."

Sultan laughed. "You awright, Bubba, you know dat?"

I mumbled some thanks for this high praise from a pimp, and Sultan ordered me to call him the next day with another report on my progress. Then he hung up.

This time, the accursed phone didn't even let me lie down.

I barked a hello into it, and Felicia Quattlebaum said from the other end of the line, "Bubba? Are you all right?"

"Sultan Sweeney says I am."

"What?"

"Never mind. I'm a little out of sorts at the moment. I nearly became dog food today."

"What are you talking about?"

"Nothing, nothing. I'm just babbling. How are you?"

"Fine, I guess." She sounded puzzled. "I was calling to see if we're going to have dinner again tonight. It is Friday, and I haven't heard from you."

"Oh, right. Sorry. I've been hot on the trail of the murderers, and I've let the time get away from me."

Better not to mention I was trying to sleep before the sun had set outside. She wouldn't see much initiative in that.

"Hot on the trail, huh? Well, you're probably doing better than me. I've been busy all day writing about Stoney Davis."

"Stoney Davis? The guy who's running for Dudley's seat?"

"Yeah. Haven't you heard the news?"

"No. All I've heard is people giving me a hard time."

"God, you're cranky today, aren't you?"

"Just tired."

"Well, for your information, well-known Democrat Stoney Davis gets his obituary on the front page tomorrow."

That got my attention. "Somebody killed him?"

"Nope. Heart attack on the Los Altos Golf Course in front of a dozen witnesses. Ambulance drove right out on the fairway, but it looks like he was dead before he hit the ground."

"Jeez. So what does that mean for the election?"

"It means the Democrats have nobody running now, unless they can put together a write-in campaign between now and November. If Dudley beats Gutierrez in the primary, he's in again."

"Terrific," I said flatly.

"My feelings exactly. Anyway, that's what I've been doing. Are we going out or not?"

I flexed my shoulders to see how many pains rippled through my body.

"I don't think so, sweetie. I've had a tough day."

"Oh, okay." She sounded disappointed, which gave me another little pain to carry around. "Well, why don't you get some rest? You can't work all the time."

"I was just thinking that very thing."

"Okay, then." She paused, reluctant to hang up. "How about breakfast tomorrow? You want to come over to my place? I could cook."

It was a rare and wonderful thing for Felicia to offer to cook. Her Indiana farm-girl upbringing shone through in the kitchen. I even put on some pounds when she was living with me and we were writing the Book. But she hadn't cooked for me lately. Most of the time, she survives on doughnuts and carry-out Chinese.

I agreed, and we set a time, and she released me from the telephone line. I eased back onto the bed and closed my eyes.

The telephone rang. I clenched my teeth and growled unintelligible curses and snatched it up.

"What?!"

"Meestah Bubba. This is Bongo speaking. Your telephone has been busy a very long time."

"Tell me about it."

"What?"

"Just an expression, Bongo. What's up?"

"Two officers of the police came around asking about you. I am of the opinion that this is something you would want very much to know."

"You bet I do." I sat up, looked around for a pen. "Who were they? What did they want?"

"It was those two tough guys from Vice. You know the ones of which I speak? One of them has an eye that looks everywhere?"

"Borkum and Bates."

"Yes, yes. They asked me many, many questions about you, how long you have lived here, do you receive a lot of visitors, that nature of thing."

"Anything else?"

"They asked me about some dates, whether I'd seen you on certain particular days. One in the month of March, one in the month of April, I believe. I told them, to me, all days seem the same. I am here every day, doing the same things."

"Good answer." I could guess which dates they'd asked about. The ones I'd written in my notebook when I went to see Romero, the days the hookers were killed.

"Then they went away. But I saw them around here later, just driving through the parking lot, then away. I found that exceedingly strange."

"Me, too, pal. But don't worry. I'll keep an eye out."

"Okay, Meestah Bubba. I will be seeing you later, aggravator."

I can never tell whether Bongo is pulling my leg.

I hung up and slowly lay back against the pillows, glaring at the telephone, daring it to ring again. I must've put the mojo on it, because it sat silent, cowed. I closed my eyes and exhaled loudly and went to sleep so fast it was like I'd blown my consciousness toward the ceiling instead of more hot air.

It was dark when the telephone rang next. I'd slept just long enough for my battered body to become stiff as an autopsy table. I grated to an upright position and fumbled for the receiver.

"Hullo?"

"Bubba Mabry?"

"Yeah?"

"This is Ralph Wartkin."

"Ralph . . . ?"

"You should know me. You seem to know my wife well enough."

"Your wife?"

"Belinda. She used to be Belinda Melville."

Belinda Wartkin? Whew.

"Yeah, I know Belinda, but I don't know what that has to do with you, or why you're calling me up in the middle of the night."

"I'll tell you why, smart guy. I want you to stay away from her."

I thought I could hear a woman's voice in the background. Belinda, probably, pleading with Ralph to hang up the phone.

"I just asked her some questions."

"I don't care what you did. I know your kind, buddy boy. You'd be all over her in a minute if she let down her guard. I may be retired, but I can still take care of what's mine—"

"Take it easy, Ralph. You're getting all bent out of shape over nothing."

"Don't tell me what's nothing. You just stay away from her."

The connection broke with a clatter, and I hung up the phone and flopped back on the bed. Just what I need, I thought. I've got a pimp and a few murders and some missing dolls and a girlfriend who stays mad at me most of the time. I was due a jealous husband.

I drifted off, splayed across the bed beside a jumble of sheets and blankets. I dreamt of answering services and car phones and a real office somewhere across town. In my dream I finally found some peace at home. My bedside table was empty, the ugly black phone gone. And I slept the sleep of the innocents.

The phone rang once more, late. It was too dark to see my clock, but I could somehow tell it was after midnight. I started to let the answering machine get it, but a phone call late at night sometimes means somebody died, and you have to answer.

"I'm gonna say this once." The voice was low, gruff, menacing. "Drop your investigation, or you'll be the next one who turns up dead."

The phone clicked to a dial tone. I held the humming receiver in my hand a long time, trying to identify the voice, telling myself I'd really heard it. It would've been reassuring for the call to have been a nightmare. But it was real.

I had trouble getting back to sleep.

10

I stood under the shower a long time the next morning. I needed a three-day soak and a stout-fingered masseuse, but a shower would have to do.

I creaked around my room, drinking coffee and putting Band-Aids around each of my fingers, which were scratched and purple from the fence wire. My thumbs were okay. If any hitchhiking came up, I was ready.

It had been more than a week since I'd done laundry, and the pickings were slim in my closet. Yesterday's jeans were wearable, once I beat the dust out of them, and I found a plaid shirt that didn't reek too strongly. I threw the dog-ripped blue shirt in the wastebasket. Let the maid wonder about that one.

As I stood before the mirror, combing my hair over the thin spots, I wondered whether Felicia had more than breakfast in mind. I hoped not. Too sore to do anything more than lie there.

Outside, a few clouds drifted low in an endless blue sky, and the sunlight bounced brightly off the chrome in the parking lot. I immediately went back inside for my sunglasses. I hadn't drunk enough the night before for a hangover, but the sun gave me that same kind of dull ache in my forehead. It hurt to squint.

Avoiding the freeway, I poked along surface roads to Felicia's place in the Heights, past plastic signs and parking lots and lawn sprinklers dancing in the sunshine.

Felicia's apartment is in one of those four-hundred-unit stucco monstrosities surrounded by baby trees and acres of asphalt. All the units look the same, which always makes me wonder how the drunks find their way home at night.

Felicia looked like she was dressed for bowling when she answered the door. Baggy pants topped by an oversized Hawaiian shirt splashed with impossibly orange orchids. But her hair was freshly brushed and she'd put on a little eye makeup and she smiled prettily when she saw me.

She ushered me in with a quick kiss. I trailed her to the apartment's tiny kitchen, which looked like the aftermath of a Three Stooges pie fight.

When Felicia's in a cooking frenzy, she manages to drag out every pan and spoon and sack of flour in the kitchen, piling them up on the countertops until the room's a dizzy, teetering maze of dirty dishes and steaming skillets and empty egg cartons. To her, a kitchen is like an artist's studio, where the creative process flows. You worry about cleaning up some other time.

When I cook, which isn't often, I put away everything as soon as I'm done with it, so there's very little cleanup after I've filled my belly. That's all the close quarters of my tiny kitchenette allow. This difference had been a point of contention when Felicia and I shared my room. One of many.

Felicia's kitchen connects to the dining room with the standard waist-high counter, and I sat on a bar stool so I could watch her play whirling dervish.

She appeared to be making omelets, though what was in the skillet was bubbling and viscous and dotted with bright red and green chunks. From a distance, it looked like a molten Christmas cookie.

Felicia poured me a mug of hot coffee and located the sugar bowl among the countertop clutter. I dumped in some sugar, saw she was occupied with the stove, and gave the coffee a quick stir with my finger rather than go into that kitchen to find a spoon.

"So, how are you doing?" she said over her shoulder.

"I'm pretty beat up. I had to outrun a big dog and jump over a fence high as this ceiling."

She turned to look me over, a dripping spatula in her hand.

"This morning?"

"Yesterday. That's why I was so weird when you called. I was still sort of in shock."

"Did this dog bite you somewhere?"

"No, I just fell a long way and landed on my ass. My vertebrae probably look like a train wreck."

"Poor baby." She turned to the stove and did some sort of martial arts move with the spatula. "Did you take some aspirin?"

"Lots."

"Good. Now we'll fill you up with some of Mama Felicia's gourmet omelets and some French toast with strawberries and powdered sugar and you'll be just fine."

"I feel better already."

Something went bing in the kitchen, a timer hidden somewhere among the battered bowls and stacked pans. She whipped open the oven and reached in with a mitt for a pan of croissants that looked crispy and light as paper lamp shades.

Felicia dumped them onto a plate, whirled to set it on the counter. She located the butter dish and a knife and said, "Dig in. They're store-bought, but they're warm."

She turned back to her cooking while I tore bread and buttered it and popped it into my mouth.

"So where did you encounter this dog?"

"It belongs to Rosie Corona."

"Rosie Corona? What were you seeing her about?"

"Oh, no, you don't. I know what you're up to."

"What?"

"You're pumping me for information. You're trying to see what I'm doing in my investigation, see if there's anything you can use. I haven't forgotten our little wager."

"Oh, yeah." She turned to me, holding greasy fingers out away from her clothes. She pushed up her glasses with the back of her wrist. "I wanted to talk to you about that."

"Backing out, eh?" It was out of my mouth before I could stop it. She gave me a hard look.

"Not exactly. If you want to keep it up, that's fine with me. But I was thinking it certainly is silly for us to be competing when we could be helping each other."

"I was thinking that, too," I lied. I'd been downright panicky about beating her in the investigation game.

"That idiot Whitworth won't let me pursue all the angles anyway. I might as well help you."

I knew better than to get her started on her fire-breathing city editor.

"So what have you got?"

She had her back to me, her elbows winging away as she performed some hocus-pocus over the stove. She slid the hot, quivering omelet from the pan onto a plate, set it in front of me, and turned immediately back to some other emergency in a skillet.

"I'm busy with this," she said. "You tell first."

A tiny *aha!* of distrust whispered in my head. A truce was going to be tough. I'd already gotten used to the idea of competitive secrecy.

"You'll show me yours if I show you mine?" I said. Just making sure.

She shot me a grin over her shoulder. "Right."

I began hesitantly, still awkward with sharing. But I soon warmed to the task, and told her about my conversations with Steve Romero and Belinda Melville. I told her about Borkum and Bates. I told her about Rosie Corona and her big dog and her pistol.

"There's something going on between Sultan Sweeney and Rosie Corona," I concluded. "They hate each other. Apparently, Rosie helped some of Sultan's girls get out of the business."

Felicia finished arranging her own plate, and came around the counter to sit on the other stool.

"Well, I wouldn't be surprised if Sweeney's threatened her," she said. "Rosie Corona and her ideas could end up making pimps an endangered species. Didn't you read my stories about her?"

"Sure. But it's been a while. Refresh my memory."

Felicia gulped a forkful of French toast and got powdered sugar on her chin. The food, as expected, was wonderful.

"Let's see. Rosie's a local girl, from an old family in the valley. She fell in with the wrong crowd, dropped out of school, and started working the streets. She probably would've ended up like that girl you found dead at your motel—"

I winced.

"—but she's tough, as you found out, and she survived. She enrolled in vocational school and turned tricks at night and on weekends until she was able to get a day job. She could've abandoned that whole scene, but instead she kept in contact with the other women and began spreading the word it was possible to escape. That's how SCORE was formed."

"So she doesn't turn tricks anymore?"

Felicia gave me a withering look and turned to her plate. We ate in silence for a while, her pissed and me unsure what to say next. Finally, she set down her fork.

"Forgive the dog reference, but you're barking up the wrong tree. Rosie Corona wouldn't have anything to do with these murders. What would be her motive? She's trying to save the prostitutes, not kill them."

I had to admit she had a point.

"Most likely," she said, "you're working for the guy who killed them."

"That's what people keep telling me."

I mopped up powdered sugar with the last bite of my toast.

"I've been working an altogether different angle," Felicia announced. "I think our friends the fundamentalists have something to do with the killings."

I nodded encouragingly, a smile frozen on my face, doubt singing high notes in my head. Felicia has a tendency to see whoever she's covering as villains, spinning their dark conspiracies. It's up to her to shine the limelight on it. Everything else, she always says, is puffery.

"They're hiding something," she continued, and, click, my suspicions were confirmed, "and that idiot Whitworth won't let me confront them with it."

I wanted to slow this train before it got rolling.

"You know, Belinda Melville said something about that. She said the killer could be some holy roller gone bad. I hope that's not the case. It'll take forever for me to track him down."

"I'm not talking about some lone killer," Felicia

said. "I think they're all involved. At least in the cover-up."

"There's a cover-up?" I didn't like the way this was going at all.

"It goes all the way to the very top."

"Aw, I don't know, sweetie. That seems a little farfetched. I don't think the Bible-thumpers would break their own Commandments just to clean up the Cruise."

"Maybe not. But what if one of their own did it? Wouldn't they try to keep it a secret? Especially if the one who did it is a big name?"

Reverend Skip Jericho flashed into my mind, with his sweaty forehead and his hollow cheeks. That powerful voice mesmerizing his flock. Could there be something more than faith burning behind those black eyes?

"Rumors are flying," Felicia said. "Lot of people around City Hall are snickering about Dudley's crusade against prostitution. Seems old Quentin used to consort with a few whores."

"Dudley?" I had to adjust my thinking. Dudley's square-jawed face swam up from my memory like I'd changed channels on the TV. "I don't know, Felicia. He seemed awfully uptight to me. I can't imagine Quentin Dudley going to an all-night party."

"Uptight is right. That's the kind who fly off the handle."

"But you said he 'used to' visit hookers. What does that have to do with the murders now?"

"What if he took it up again? Say he's cracked under the pressure of campaigning and crusading. He goes to the Cruise for some firsthand 'research.' Someone as repressed as Dudley could flip out and off a hooker or three."

I didn't know what to say. There seemed to be some

question here about just who was flipping out. Felicia was flushed and her hands danced as she spun out her crazy theory.

"So, you think a city councilman—who gets his picture in the paper twice a week—could go down to the Cruise unnoticed, pick up a girl, and kill her. Not once, but three times?"

"I know it sounds odd, but they're hiding something, Bubba. I can feel it. There's something wrong with the dynamic there."

"The dynamic."

"Yeah, between Dudley and his wife and Jericho and some of the others. It all looks fervent and righteous, but there's something bubbling under the surface."

"You know, it's a long jump from something bubbling under the surface to a city councilman killing hookers with his bare hands."

"Maybe he didn't do it himself, but he knows something about it. Maybe Marilyn did it. She seems nutzoid enough to kill somebody if she found out Quentin was sleeping around and maybe bringing AIDS home to her and the kiddies."

"Two of the women were raped, Felicia. I doubt she's nutzoid enough for that."

"She could've had some man do it. Some crazy follower of Jericho's. Like those thugs who hustled that drunk away from the rally."

"Hey, I was going to ask you about that. How come you didn't mention that in your story?"

She scowled, but there was some underlying pleasure at me asking her about something she'd written. I'd scored a few points.

"I put it in, and that idiot Whitworth took it out. He's always doing stuff like that. And now he says I can't approach Dudley about my suspicions."

"You told your boss about this?"

"Yeah, a big mistake. I should've just gone straight to Dudley without telling Whitworth first. Like they say, 'It's easier to get forgiveness than permission.'"

I could imagine Whitworth's reaction, even though I'd never met him. Conspiracy-hunters like Felicia are the ones who get newspapers into legal battles.

"That's why I want you to do it," she said.

"Do what?"

"Go see Dudley. Feel around. See what you can turn up."

"Me?"

"Yeah, you. I can't do it, but you could."

"Oh, I don't know, hon. I don't even know the man. I'm just going to go into his office and accuse him of murder?"

"Not accuse. Just talk to him. See if he knows anything. You can poke around the edges without getting him stirred up."

"You think so?" This was perhaps the first time she'd attributed any sort of prowess to me, other than the obligatory compliments in bed. I wasn't nearly so flattered this time.

"Sure. Why don't you give him a call? I've got his number."

She got up to fetch the phone, and I wondered how long she'd had this planned. When the breakfast offer occurred to her? Maybe earlier, when she first cooked up the idea of us racing the case to a conclusion? I didn't like it one bit.

She handed me the cordless phone and a slip of paper with Dudley's number written on it. Her eyes shone with excitement.

"Is this his office or home number?" I asked her.

"Office. His home number's unlisted."

Not very likely he's going to be at his office, I

thought. Not on a Saturday morning. He's home with his kids, watching Bible story videos. I dialed. It rang once.

"This is Quentin Dudley."

"Oh, uh, hi, Mr. Dudley." I goggled my eyes at Felicia, and she covered her mouth with her hand. "My name's Bubba Mabry, and I'm a private investigator and, uh, I'd like to talk to you."

"A private investigator?"

"Yes, sir."

"What's this about?"

"I'd rather talk in person, if that's possible." Mostly, I just wanted to squirm out of this call.

"I'm campaigning from lunch until near midnight. But I'll be at my office for another hour. I could see you for a few minutes."

"Just a second." I covered the mouthpiece and whispered to Felicia. "He wants me to come right now."

"So, go, *go.*"

Despite a sinking feeling in my chest, I said into the receiver, "I'll be right there."

He told me how to find his office and we hung up.

Felicia danced around me like an excited poodle.

"Oh, boy," she said. "This is going to be fun."

Yeah, I thought, oh boy.

11

I parked in the dank underground lot beneath Civic Plaza, and located the tunnel that connects to City Hall. During the week, you can rarely find a parking space there, all of them taken early by city workers and cops and lawyers. On a Saturday, it's spooky. The garage is so empty every step rings out. Through the tunnel into the darkened building, as silent as a tomb for the ghosts of old bureaucrats.

The escalators were shut off for the weekend, so I climbed them like stairs and was met at the top by a chunky Hispanic guard. I told him where I was going, and he used a phone to clear it with Dudley. I stood whistling through my teeth, rocking from heel to toe, wondering what the hell I was doing there.

The guard hung up the phone, gave me a final going-over with his dark eyes, then told me to go on up.

The elevators were working, at least, and I stepped out onto the ninth floor, into a waiting room ringed by offices. The reception desk was empty, but I could hear a few muffled voices and a lone typewriter clacking away somewhere. I found Dudley's office, took a deep breath and knocked.

"Come in."

The room smelled like lemons. Quentin Dudley stood behind his desk in his shirtsleeves, a spray can of furniture polish in one hand and a soft rag in the other, rubbing with the grain of his broad mahogany desk.

"Bubba Mabry?"

I shook his hand, which felt oily and soft and probably was lemon-scented, too. He gestured me toward a chair, staring at the Band-Aids on my fingers but not saying anything about them.

"Excuse the mess. Saturday is the one time in the week I can get things straightened up around here."

I'd never seen an office so orderly. Not a loose paper clip in the place, and the in and out trays were empty and dustless. Even the rubber plant in the corner was symmetrical and shiny.

I smoothed my hair with my hand. So much neatness made me feel shabby and disheveled. I crossed my legs and tried to relax.

Dudley put away his cleaning equipment and sat very straight in his high-backed leather chair. He was trim and muscular, with wide, knobby hands that rested on the chair's arms. He wore a blue shirt and black slacks and, as a concession to it being Saturday, had loosened his dark tie ever so slightly.

"So, Mr. Mabry, what can I do for you?"

I pictured Dudley's big hands tossing me from his office, then the thick-necked guard downstairs pitching me the rest of the way to my car.

"Well, uh, I'm investigating some murders down on Central Avenue, and I thought you might be able to help me."

"Murders? What would I know about murders?"

"Maybe nothing. But you might be able to tell me about some people who would know something."

"I doubt it. City councilmen don't usually get mixed up in such things, Mr. Mabry. Especially at election time."

"I understand that. But maybe you could answer just a few questions for me, then I'll be on my way and you can get back to pressing the flesh."

The words clanked in my ears—any mention of flesh was probably not the way to start this—but I pressed ahead.

"See, the murders I'm looking into are the killings of those hookers. You know all about them because of your crusade, right?"

"I read the newspapers," he said. "Beyond that, I don't—"

"I was thinking, with all the publicity about the crusade, maybe some crazy has decided to take hellfire-and-brimstone into his own hands. Know what I mean?"

The muscles bulged above Dudley's wide jawbone.

"First of all, Mr. Mabry, this sounds like a matter for the police, so I probably shouldn't even be talking to you. Secondly, I hope you're not trying to say someone in our movement is responsible for those killings. They're law-abiding, God-fearing people. None of them would commit murder, and I wouldn't know anything about it if someone had."

"Has anyone been acting strange? Have you heard anything about somebody who's maybe a little too fervent?"

"No. I can assure you, Mr. Mabry, you're looking in the wrong place. Those killings are sinners turning on one another, not the work of some Christian gone awry."

"How can you be so sure?"

Dudley rocked to his feet and turned his back to me, stepping over to the window, which looked out onto an office tower across the street. He thought it over for a minute.

"Have you ever heard the term anomie?" he asked over his shoulder.

I shook my head.

"It means someone, or some culture, that's lost its social controls. A person with this illness has no moral code, no sense of right and wrong or how to interact with others so we all get along."

"All right." I wasn't sure where this was leading, but I'm always willing to learn something.

"When it's a culture or subculture that's suffering from anomie, then you have anarchy. People preying on each other. That's the blight we have on Central Avenue."

My cheeks warmed. "Now don't you think you're sort of lumping everybody together? I happen to live on East Central—"

"Then you know exactly what I'm talking about." He plunked into his chair to punctuate his point.

"So that makes it okay to kill hookers?"

"Absolutely not." There was something soft around the edges of his lipless mouth, something that said eliminating hookers might not be such a bad idea. "But if the police crack down hard enough, then the trade eventually will die.

"If you live down there, Mr. Mabry, then I'd think you'd support our movement. Every layer of the criminal element we remove should cause others to move on. We stop prostitution—which is so open that it's easy to make arrests—and a lot of the drug-dealing and petty crime down there will dry up, too."

He had me at a disadvantage. He'd been polishing his argument in front of Kiwanis luncheons and

Junior League teas for months. I hadn't given it all that much thought.

"You know," I said after a few seconds' pondering, "it's not the criminals who provide the hookers' clientele. Hell, there aren't enough criminals to keep them in business. It's teenagers and tourists and people from the Nosebleed Heights."

I didn't think he could get any stiffer, but he arched his spine and his eyebrows at my making fun of his district. I was just getting warmed up.

"Yeah, hookers have told me stories about kinky ministers and lonely businessmen and cops. Even city councilmen. You'd be surprised who hits the Cruise. Or maybe you wouldn't . . ."

Dudley's face flushed red, but his voice was low and cold. "What the hell is that supposed to mean?"

I tried to look coy. "Well, there have been rumors. . . ."

He bounced to his feet and leaned across the desk. "Are you insinuating something, Mabry?"

"Now I never said—"

"Do these rumors have something to do with me?"

"It's just something I heard—"

"From whom?"

"I can't say."

He straightened up, sneering. "Of course you can't. Because there's nothing *to* say. You're a sniveling liar who's making this stuff up as he goes along."

"You know, you shouldn't talk to me that way. . . ."

I don't know what I planned to do about it. I felt pinned in my chair by his hot rage.

"Let me tell you something, buddy," he said, his breath coming hard. "I live the cleanest life of anybody in this building. If you *ever* say to anyone that I've had anything to do with prostitutes, and I hear about it, I'll sue your ass off. And when we get done in court, I'll own everything you have and everything you ever hope to have. Got me?"

I nodded, tried not to audibly gulp.

"Now get out of my office."

He turned away to the windows, breaking off any chance for further conversation. His shoulders trembled and he clenched his fists beside his thighs.

I considered it an honorable retreat since he didn't watch me slink out.

I closed the door ever so quietly and stood in the waiting room for a few moments, reeling in my scattered thoughts. I should know better than to get into an argument with a politician. They get so much practice.

One thing I was sure about: it was all Felicia's fault. I was being threatened with lawsuits by one of Albuquerque's leading citizens just because she had a bug up her butt about his crusade.

"Bubba! What are you doing here?"

My eyes snapped into focus and there was squat Alice Burden, glaring up at me from under the brim of a broad green felt hat. A stuffed pigeon spread its wings around the crown, speared in place with two large hat pins. Glass eyes gave the bird a surprised look, like maybe it had splatted there while Alice was riding in a convertible.

"Why, uh, hello, Alice."

"Get into my office right now."

She herded me through a door and into her office, which was cluttered and smelly compared to Dudley's monastic cell. I stumbled along in a daze, my ears still ringing with the councilman's fury.

After she closed the door, Alice pounced.

"What in the world could you be thinking, Bubba? What are you doing, hanging around the hallway like a bat? Do you think I want the rest of the council to know you're working for me? That's just the sort of horny dilemma I need, everyone knowing about my little indiscretion with a carny."

The pigeon bobbed and swooped on top of the hat as her jaws flapped.

"Hold on, Alice, hold on."

"Don't tell *me* to hold on, Bubba. I'm madder than a wet hornet. This was supposed to be a *confidential* investigation!"

"Well, it's not going to be confidential if you keep hollering about it!"

That tripped her up.

"Nobody's going to connect me to your old romance. As far as anyone else knows, it's just a valuable doll collection."

"Well, don't you think you hanging around City Hall is going to raise some questions—"

"I wasn't even here to see you, Alice."

"Wh-What?"

"I was down the hall, talking to Quentin Dudley."

"Dudley? What for?"

"Another confidential investigation."

Alice's indignation evaporated. "Oh, come on, Bubba. You can tell me."

"Nope. Then you wouldn't trust me to keep your secrets."

"Sure I will."

"Now, Alice—"

"Wait, you don't have to tell me. You told me on the phone. You're investigating those murders."

"Well, yeah—"

"You think Dudley has something to do with them?"

"Lord, no. I never said—"

"Tell me, Bubba, or I'll have to assume the worst."

I ran my hand over my face in exasperation. "Don't

go assuming anything. It looks like a false lead. Some rumor about Dudley and hookers. I never really believed it."

Dudley had reacted strongly, though, hadn't he? A little too strongly? Wouldn't a smooth politician be more accustomed to deflecting any accusation? Why did he get so mad so quick?

"Dudley and hookers, eh?" Alice said, breaking my chain of thought before I could forge a good link. "That's going back a lot of years."

"What do you mean?"

"This story about Dudley. When he was in high school, right?"

"I'm not sure we're talking about the same story. You go ahead."

Alice looked me over before speaking. I tried not to stare at the bird.

"When Dudley was in high school," she began, "he was one of those kids who had everything. Rich parents, good looks, big star athlete, always doing church work. Other kids called him Dudley Do-right. A perfect record except for one brush with the law."

She paused, looked at me out of the corner of her eye to make sure I was rapt. I nodded eagerly.

"One night he got a little drunk with some of his football buddies, who I think were probably out to convert old Do-right. Anyhow, he ended up in a motel room with a hooker. Something went wrong, and he flipped his rug, and he nearly beat the poor girl to death. If one of his friends hadn't kicked in the door and pulled him off her, it would've been murder."

My mouth was dry from gaping, and I closed it and swallowed.

"How come I've never heard this before?"

"Because it was twenty years ago. And because Quentin's father did a terrific job of shutting it all up. He kept it out of the newspapers with a few phone calls, and he paid off the girl, paid all her medical bills, too, and she dropped the charges. As far as the official record is concerned, it never happened."

"But you know about it."

"I hear most everything. And I forget nothing."

No wonder the mention of Alice Burden's name gives everyone in city government the trembles.

"So," she said, "that's obviously not the story you were checking out. What have you heard?"

I snapped to. Time to get dancing again.

"Well, like I said, nothing concrete. You know, rumors."

"Like what?"

Oh, to hell with it.

"To tell you the truth, Alice, I don't want to say. Dudley said if I ever repeated it, he'd sue me."

She put her fists on her broad hips and cocked her head to squint up at me. The pigeon seemed to stare from the same angle.

"Don't you think you can trust me? I won't tell anyone."

The hell you won't.

"I went to see him because I thought somebody in the crusade might've wigged out, you know, and offed those hookers. But he didn't know anything."

One eyebrow slid up her forehead. "And?"

"And what?"

"What else? That wouldn't be enough for Dudley to threaten you with a suit."

She had me there.

"Well, I sorta suggested he might visit hookers himself."

A laugh rumbled up from within Alice's thick body, made her jowls jiggle like Jell-O. It erupted from her mouth in a Broadway bray that rattled the windows. She laughed for a long time. I crossed my arms over my chest and tried to look pissed.

"I'm sorry, Bubba." She wiped her eyes. "I can tell you weren't joking, but I couldn't help laughing. The idea of Quentin Dudley lying down with whores is funnier than a pig on carpet."

"You just said that when he was in high school—"

"Oh, hell, Bubba, that was high school. We all did things in high school we're not proud of. You know about some of mine."

"I'm still looking for your dolls, Alice."

"Oh, I know, honey, don't worry about that. I can tell you're busier than a one-legged man in a sack race. Lord knows, if you're going to go stirring things up around here, I'll wait my turn. I can hardly wait to see what you'll do next."

"It won't be anything to do with Quentin Dudley, I'll tell you that."

She found a box of tissues on her desk and wiped her eyes and honked her nose.

"That's probably just as well," she said. "I don't think Quentin knows anything that will help you. And I certainly don't think he whores around. Not with his history."

She paused, like she was remembering something.

"I've often thought that incident in high school may be what propels Quentin and Marilyn in their crusade. Like wiping out prostitution could erase Quentin's past."

"Doesn't work that way."

"You said it, Bubba."

12

I spend most of my time trying to convince people I'm Sam Spade, and instead I come off like Gomer Pyle. I try to conceal something, I'm transparent. I try to be sly, I trip over my own feet. I'm a freaking goof. Such thoughts kicked me down the City Hall escalator and back to my car.

I wandered around Downtown, sitting at one red light after another, replaying the City Council conversations in my head.

If what Alice said was true, Quentin Dudley had beaten up at least one hooker in his life. Why not more? Maybe the pressure of campaigning and crusading *had* gotten to him, had sent him out to repeat the One Big Sin of his youth.

I shook my head to clear the thoughts. Who was I kidding? Quentin Dudley? City Councilman Quentin Dudley? Dropping into cheap motels to slice and dice a whore or two? Get real.

That Alice would repeat the high school story to someone like me showed just how insanely ballsy she could be. What if she was in Dudley's office right now, confronting him with the rumor I'd repeated? The thought of a summons arriving at my door gave me a loose feeling in my bowels.

I steered the Chevy into a diagonal parking slot on Central Avenue and cut the engine. Lindy's, a Downtown institution, was just down the street, and they had a bathroom there if I needed it. I swallowed hard, rested my head back on the seat, and, with an effort, gained control of all bodily functions. My breathing slowed. I dried my sweaty palms on my jeans.

Even with the window down, it started getting hot in the car. The wind that had whipped the town senseless for weeks had vanished. Without it, Albuquerque heats up in a hurry. At one mile's elevation, the sun's light is white and bright, and you can almost feel future skin cancers bubbling up on your arms. I got out of the car and found some shade on the sidewalk.

Downtown, Central Avenue is a different world from the one where I live. Out on East Central, everything was built in the fifties and it all has that neon-lit, streamlined chrome, tail-fin Cadillac look. But Downtown, Central looks old and weary—two-story brick buildings with ornate false fronts, toothless old cars limping along, toupees of black asphalt patching potholes.

Closer inspection revealed the windowless storefront I leaned against was a porn shop, a branch office of the Newsworld shops on East Central. Just where I wanted to be seen hanging around. I moseyed on down the dusty sidewalk toward Lindy's, keeping to the shade.

I sat at the counter and ordered a Coke. The café was empty except for a trio of old men nursing coffees near the door. Granted, it was a Saturday, when no office workers are Downtown, but the lack of customers made me sad. Not that I wanted a crowd buzzing around me while I tried to think, but the old-fashioned counter and the padded booths made me sentimental for a time in Albuquerque I'd never known. Before the freeways came, when everyone going west to California drove along Route 66 through the heart of the city. When there were no malls, and the locals still found reason to go Downtown. When places like the Desert Breeze Motor Lodge represented the Latest in Family Traveling Convenience. In those round-fendered days, I'd still been in Mississippi, growing up in the country, living in the shadow of my mother's limelight.

Not now, I thought. This is no time to start obsessing on the Cutwaller gullibility. I've overcome that. I can't be fooled as long as I approach each investigation carefully, looking at everything like I've never seen it before.

I pondered Dudley some more, but that made the soda burble in my belly. Even the thought of the points I'd scored with Felicia did nothing to ease my apprehension. But it did give me an idea of what to do next.

I paid my tab and borrowed a phone book from a swarthy guy behind the cash register. Then I limped out into the heat to a corner pay phone and dialed the number I'd looked up.

Even though things had gone badly with Dudley, I wasn't willing to give up the angle of a Bible-thumper being the killer. If not Dudley himself, then maybe one of the other crazies in his crusade. It might turn into a dead end, but it beat any other lead I had. And it would get me in good with Felicia.

Reverend Skip Jericho answered with a booming "Hello."

I burped my way through an introduction and told him what I wanted.

"Frankly, Mr. Mabry, I'm in the middle of composing tomorrow's sermon. Could this wait until Monday?"

"I'd rather not. It'll only take a few minutes."

He sighed and agreed. I told him I'd be there in fifteen minutes.

Reverend Skip lived on the West Mesa, at the city's western frontier, where sunbaked houses circle cul-de-sacs like covered wagons. Each neighborhood is a pod of humanity ringed by "unimproved desert," like you could improve on something so fragile and unadorned.

Felicia told me once that living in the desert is like living by the ocean. Humbling. You're surrounded by an environment that's, at best, unfriendly to man. At worst, it's deadly. Because it's inhospitable, it stays beautiful and unspoiled. You live your urban life, but in the distance you can always see the edges, where Nature takes over.

I doubt people who live on those edges see it that way. They probably just curse the sand they sweep out of their homes.

Albuquerque once was confined to the green oasis of the Rio Grande valley. But once the Sun Belt boomed, slapped-together houses climbed up the volcanic mesa west of the river. They spread so rapidly the government had to race to declare the dead volcanoes a nature park before somebody built something on them.

Jericho lived in one of the newest developments, a walled compound off a freshly paved section of Unser Boulevard. Build a place on high ground so you have a view of the distant mountains, then throw up a wall around it so you can't see anything. Probably kept the blowing sand at bay, though.

It was a nice house for a preacher, all white stucco and big windows and red tile, and I wondered whether the congregation provided it for him free of charge, like some do, or whether Jericho had pocketed enough to buy it outright.

Jericho answered the door in jeans and a golf shirt. Without the black suit, he looked even slighter, but his handshake was like a nutcracker, and his voice was deeper than God's.

"Welcome, Mr. Mabry. Come on in."

The house had ceilings high enough to echo, but the living room furniture was bulky plaid stuff that had discount store written all over it. Sliding glass doors looked out onto a sandy backyard just big enough to hold a swing set.

"Can I offer you a glass of water?"

"No, thanks. I never touch the stuff."

He didn't smile. His skin stretched so tight over his bony skull, there wasn't room for a smile. His face might crack.

"This won't take but a minute, Reverend. Then you can get back to your sermonizing."

"That's fine. Cheryl and the kids are at the mall until three or so. She tries to keep everybody out of the house on Saturdays to give me time to think."

"Well, sorry to butt in, but I'm working on a case that's pretty urgent. Somebody's killing prostitutes along Central Avenue, as you know, and I'm trying to find them and stop it."

Jericho sat back in his chair and crossed his skinny legs, looking so calm he might take to whittling any second.

"An admirable goal. It's a disgrace what's been happening on Central, and the police don't seem to be getting anywhere."

"Yeah, well, I haven't gotten very far either. Which is why I came to see you."

"You think I can help?"

"Well, I hope so. See, I was thinking that whoever killed those girls must have a screw loose, if you'll, uh, pardon the expression. And it occurred to me somebody like that might also be attracted to your crusade. You know, a hanger-on, somebody who's a little too religious for his own good."

Jericho's expression sharpened while I bumbled around. "You think it's possible to be too religious?"

My mother's face flashed through my mind, her eyes closed, her lips moving in silent prayer. Damned right it's possible.

"You know what I mean. Somebody who's off his rocker. Sometimes, they're attracted to movements."

He nodded. "That's true. But I can assure you no one like that is involved in what we're trying to do on Central Avenue."

"How can you be so sure?"

"I know my people like a shepherd knows his flock. There are no wolves among them."

Nice imagery, but it came a little too easily. I would've felt better if he'd at least taken a moment to think it over.

"It's funny you should stop by here today, Mr. Mabry. The sermon I'm writing for tomorrow is about Central Avenue."

Oh, shit.

"You see, I know something of Central Avenue and the sin down there. I once was like you, wallowing in sin, living among painted women and petty thieves."

I hadn't said anything about living on Central, had I? Had I said something about it on the phone? I couldn't remember.

"One day I woke up in a cheap motel with a woman I didn't know. I had a hangover and I couldn't remember anything from the night before."

That did sound familiar.

"I went into the bathroom and threw up. Then I looked at myself in the mirror. I was shocked by what

I saw. I looked ten years older than I was. I was pale and my eyes were bloodshot and I needed a shave."

He paused and waited for me to nod, to show him I was caught up in his tale.

"And that's when God spoke to me."

Yikes.

"They were not soft words, not gentle words. They were harsh and cold. He told me I was a sinner, that my heart had grown as black as a smoker's lungs. The way to redemption, He said, was to repent and to help others do the same."

I shifted on the sofa, thinking of that old joke about the city slicker visiting the fervent hillbillies who handle rattlesnakes to show their piety:

"Where's the back door?"

"Ain't one."

"Where do you want one?"

A righteous fire burned in Jericho's eyes. The longer he talked, rehearsing his sermon, the deeper and louder his voice boomed. I'd seen this sort of thing before, growing up in church, but it had been a lot of years. It gave me the heebies.

"Perhaps the real reason you came to see me, Mr. Mabry, is that you, too, are tired of lying down in Sin."

"How's that?"

"Would you like to kneel down with me?"

"Kneel?"

"To pray, Mr. Mabry. We could pray together, both for your Salvation and for Divine guidance in your investigation."

My feet danced, headed toward the door. I remained seated through sheer force of will.

"I, um, don't think that'll be necessary, Reverend."

"Aren't you concerned about eternal damnation?"

I rubbed my hands on my knees, trying to erase

some of the tension building up inside me. Trying not to bolt.

"I'm more concerned with the here-and-now."

"Eternity is a long time, Mr. Mabry."

"The longest. Look, I really just want to know whether you have any idea who might be killing those girls."

"Any idea? Certainly, I have an idea, Mr. Mabry."

Okay, now we're getting somewhere. I leaned forward, ready to hear his theory. He did the same, tilting forward conspiratorially, until our faces were only inches apart.

"It's Satan."

"Aw, jeez." I rocked back from him like he'd sneezed. "Come on, Reverend. That's not what I need to hear."

"It's exactly what you should hear, Mr. Mabry. Satan is behind these killings, just like he's behind the rest of the sin that lines the gutters of Central Avenue."

The back of my neck felt suddenly hot, and I tugged at my collar to let some air in there.

"So I should just keep an eye out for some guy with horns and a pointy tail, and that'll be my killer?"

Jericho leaned back and gave me a tut-tut look.

"Satan doesn't walk the streets. He's *inside* people. The evil urges every man sometimes feels welling up inside, that's Satan. Someone who's given in to those urges, who's surrendered himself to the Devil's work, that will be the murderer."

"And the people in your crusade don't have these urges?"

"Everyone has them, Mr. Mabry. Keeping them in check, keeping to a righteous path, that's the struggle we all face."

"What if I told you one of your crusaders had lost the struggle?"

130

That slowed him up.

"I'd be interested to hear about that. Maybe I could help."

Quentin Dudley's warning screamed in my brain, made me stumble.

"Let's just say there are rumors circulating that one of them has been visiting hookers."

"Rumors? You know, spreading rumors is a sin, Mr. Mabry."

"So's cutting up hookers."

Jericho tucked his chin in a half nod, waiting.

"That's really all I ought to say about it."

"You're not going to say who it is?"

"I don't want to sin here in your home by spreading rumors."

"If you know something concrete, I'd like to hear it. You're going to leave me worrying about everyone in my congregation."

"You just better worry the newspapers don't get hold of it."

I stood up, began thanking him for his time. But he wasn't listening. The mention of newspapers had him thinking. Then dawn glinted in his eye and he looked at me with new interest, like I'd proven I was something more than just another lost soul.

He said nothing more about the murders as he walked me to the door, but something in his manner, an excitement, an eagerness, told me he could use the information I'd given him. Just what I needed, I thought, another person who might confront Dudley with my gossip. No way the councilman would believe I'd only leaked hints and innuendo. I might as well buy a billboard along I-40 and print the whole damned thing up there.

It was hot in the Chevy, and I rolled down the windows and cranked up the engine. The air conditioner blew air hot enough to dry laundry. While I waited for it to cool down, I thought about what I'd said to Jericho, how much I'd given away. And what did I get in return? A sermon on that bad old Devil man.

That, and one other thing. I'd gotten Jericho to thinking, wondering what I had on his golden boy. That might not do my case any good, but it stirred Felicia's pot for her. And that was worth something.

13

I was nearly home when I saw red and blue lights flashing in the parking lot of the Paradise Motel.

The Paradise isn't any older than the place where I live, but its paint is peeling and it looks tired. The motel is best known along the Cruise for its wind-damaged sign, which for years has said DISCOUNT RAT S.

Police cars filled the parking lot haphazardly, spilling their flashing lights onto the motel windows, where guests peeked out warily. Something—maybe instinct, maybe just curiosity—told me to check it out. I parked around the corner.

Thirty or forty people had gathered to gawk, herded by a uniformed cop who moved around their flanks, barking like a sheepdog.

"Okay, folks, move it along, nothing to see, stay behind the yellow tape!"

Rahr-rahr-rahr-rar-rar. His face was red from the effort.

I squeezed through the crowd. Near the yellow CRIME SCENE tape the gawkers had carved out a wide circle to make room for a pungent wino who'd pissed in his filthy pants. He stared blearily at the cops and the flashing lights, probably wondering whether it was all just another hallucination.

The door to one downstairs room stood open, and cops and plainclothes detectives bustled in and out like worker ants. Lieutenant Steve Romero appeared in the doorway, rubbing his hands together like he was washing them.

"Steve!"

The sweaty, red-faced officer immediately was up in my face. "Don't bother the investigators!"

Romero took a few steps in my direction, caught a whiff of the wino, and backed up. He shouted at the cop to let me through. The crowd muttered enviously as I ducked under the tape.

"What's up, Steve?"

"Another prostitute's been killed. That's number five."

"Anybody I know?"

"You should. Looks like she works for Sultan Sweeney."

I flinched.

"Her body was discovered a couple of hours ago by a girlfriend who came to take her shopping. That's her over there."

He pointed at a bony bleached blonde who stood against a car fender, hugging herself, tears streaking her mascara. She looked like Alice Cooper.

"Been dead long?"

"I'd guess four or five hours. We'll have to see what the coroner says."

Romero's guesses in such matters were good enough for me.

"And it's one of Sultan's girls? You're sure?"

"Does the name Lorrie Quintana mean anything to you?"

"Never heard of her."

"Well, the boys in Vice say she's been on Sultan's string awhile. Guess you get to be the one who tells him she's dead."

"Me? Why don't you tell him?"

Romero's gaze hardened. "Hey, Bubba, we call the next of kin. That's tough enough. We don't have to call her pimp, too."

I nodded and mumbled and scratched my ear, trying to cover my sudden anxiety. Another dead hooker is not what Sultan Sweeney would like to hear. That old saw about killing the messenger flashed through my mind like a newsreel headline.

Beyond Romero, two paramedics wheeled a body bag out of the room on a gurney. Romero heard the clatter and shouted for them to hold on a second.

"Want to take a look?" he asked me.

"Not really."

"Sure you do. Come on, Bubba. See what happens to people who work for Sultan Sweeney."

I had no choice but to follow. Romero screened the gurney from the crowd with his bearlike body, and unzipped the body bag enough that I could peek in at her face.

Lorrie Quintana had big brown eyes circled with mascara. One of them now was bigger than the other, sort of popped out like it was trying to spring from its socket. Dried blood crusted around her ears, and her lips were purple.

"The perp banged her on the head with something. We're not sure what. Maybe his fists. Whatever, it crushed her skull. He raped her, too."

I stared down into Lorrie Quintana's misshapen face.

"He came, he saw, he conked her."

"Right." Romero grinned. Cops love any joke about a stiff, but it left a bad taste in my mouth and my stomach flopped.

Romero said, "You all right?"

"Yeah, I'm okay. Corpses make me nervous, that's all."

"Good thing you don't have my job."

"You got that right."

The lieutenant nodded, and one of the paramedics zipped up the bag. Then they rolled the gurney away to a waiting ambulance. Someone inside the room shouted for Romero, and he gave me a friendly chuck on the shoulder.

"Time to get back to work. Let me know what you hear from Sweeney."

Romero left me standing in the no-man's-land on the wrong side of the yellow tape. I felt the eyes of the crowd on me, like I was being picked out of a lineup.

I turned to rejoin the crowd, and spotted the Vice Brothers, Borkum and Bates, in their matching wind-breakers on the far side of the parking lot. They muttered to each other and glared at me.

Borkum aimed his good eye at me and crooked a stubby finger to call me over. I went the other way. I didn't exactly run, but I stepped lively as I weaved through the crowd and ducked around the corner. I scrambled into the Chevy, cranked up the engine, and was gone before the Vice cops could catch up.

I circled the block and turned back onto Central Avenue, headed toward home. I took deep breaths to calm my insides. Why had Borkum and Bates been hanging around like that? Had they been waiting to see if I'd show up?

As I reached the Desert Breeze, it occurred to me they could be following. I drove on past, and went several blocks up Central, watching my mirrors. I saw nobody, so I swung into the parking lot of a convenience store. The pay phone was outside, which made me nervous, but I got Sultan Sweeney's number out of my wallet and dialed it. I kept an eye on the street while the phone rang.

"Hullo?"

"Sweeney?"

"One minute."

The blunt instrument of a voice had to belong to Sultan's pet giant, Hughie. In a second, Sultan came on the line.

"Hey, Sultan, this is Bubba Mabry."

"Yeah, Bubba. You got somethin' for me?"

"Bad news, I'm afraid. Lorrie Quintana's been killed."

There was a long silence on the line. Just when I thought I'd have to repeat myself, that there was something wrong with the phone, he said thickly, "Get over here right now."

He gave me an address and hung up.

I didn't like the way things were shaping up, but I did as I was told. Maybe Sultan Sweeney intended to fire me because another girl had been murdered before I could solve anything. That would be okay with me.

Sultan's reputation for violence worried me, though. If he was really disappointed in me, he might show it by getting rough. Or worse, by turning his decaying bodyguard loose on me. While stopped at a red light, I got my pistol out of the glove compartment and tucked it into the back of my jeans, covering it with my loose shirttail. Just in case.

Sultan Sweeney lived in a surprisingly modest house surrounded by a level green lawn and shady elms. The house was on the fringes of a swank old neighborhood known as Ridgecrest. I wondered what Sultan told his neighbors he did for a living.

Hughie opened the door, and I was immediately hit by his stench. He stepped out of the way, but I still bumped my shoulder on the doorjamb as I tried to squeeze through without touching him. Or staring at his pale lava-field skin. I'd seen enough ugliness for one day.

The house was cool and dark inside. Low, over-stuffed furniture crowded the center of the living room under a lazy ceiling fan. The Oriental rug was worth more than I make in a year. Modern art hung on the walls, all looking like someone had tried to slash the canvas with a wet paintbrush.

"Mr. Sweeney'll be out in a minute."

I sat on one of the low sofas, my back to the giant, who hovered by the door out of habit.

"He seemed upset about something." Nervousness touched his voice ever so slightly. Keeping Sultan Sweeney in a good mood was a full-time job for Hughie.

I cranked my head around to look at him, thought better of it, took a sudden interest in a nearby painting.

"Well, I'm not surprised." I tried to sound nonchalant. "Another one of his girls has been found murdered."

"Uh-oh."

Sultan Sweeney strode into the room, a drink in one hand and a cordless phone in the other. He wore a long silk robe of swirling paisley over his clothes, but he had on his pointy-toed street shoes. Like he'd just been leaving when I called. Or had just returned from somewhere.

I'd expected fierce and angry, but instead Sultan looked like he'd been crying. His eyes were red-rimmed and his nose was pink from blowing. He gave me the once-over, then gulped the last of his drink and slumped onto the sofa across from me.

"Awright, Bubba, what de hell happened?"

"Somebody bashed Lorrie Quintana in the head so hard it popped her eyes out."

Sultan didn't twitch, but behind me, Hughie made a noise like a whimper. Sultan gave him a sharp look.

"Hughie, if you're gonna stand around whinin', why don't you find somethin' else to do? Go out back and wash de car."

I sat very still as Hughie rumbled out of the room. Once he was gone, Sultan said, with a nasty edge to his voice, "Hire de fuckin' handicapped, and dat's what you get."

I said nothing. If Sultan wanted to take his grief out on Hughie, that was okay by me.

Sultan caught himself, and his features relaxed ever so slightly, and he said, "Aw, shit, I didn't mean dat. Hughie's awright. He's just soft."

I thought: soft like an old doughnut, crumbling.

"How'd he end up working for you, anyway?"

Sultan gave me a what's-it-to-you look, but he answered.

"I met Hughie right after I came to Albuquerque. I was probably de first person to ever be nice to him. It was only natural dat he'd become my eunuch."

Alarm must've registered on my face. Sultan chuckled and shook his head.

"I don't mean de boy's been castrated, Bubba. But he might as well be, you know? What woman would touch him? He's perfect for de job."

Sultan had a point. One thing a pimp doesn't need is competition from his own people. Sultan's girls stuck with him because of love and loyalty as much as money or fear. And, from the look of it, he loved them, too. Or at least he thought he did. Why else would he be grieving? Lost income can be replaced, but a lost soul's gone forever.

Just to keep talking, I said, "What's the matter with him, anyway?"

"Hughie was born with some kind of sensitive skin condition. The boy's got no immunity, I guess. He catches every skin disease. Acne, warts, boils, viruses. I've sent him to all kinds of doctors, but there's nothin' they can do."

"You don't mind the way he smells?"

Sultan smiled and touched a fingertip to his perfect nose. "Dead nerves. I can't smell shit."

I nodded, and we both fell silent. I watched Sultan's impassive face, wondering what was coming next. As I watched, the porcelain skin knitted around his eyebrows and the anticipated rage bubbled to the surface.

When he spoke, his voice was barely above a whisper. "Who's killin' my girls, Bubba?"

"I, uh, I don't really know yet. I've been following some leads, but they haven't led me to a suspect. I wouldn't even know about this Lorrie Quintana if I hadn't happened to drive up while the cops were hauling her body away."

"I'm not payin' you to 'happen' onto shit. I want you to *make* somethin' happen."

"I know, I know. I'm working on it. I'm just sorry another one of your girls had to get killed before I could sort it out."

Sultan's lips tightened. "Yeah, I'm sorry, too. At dis rate, I'll be out of bidness before you figure out anything."

It seemed wiser not to reply. Sultan rose from the low sofa and glided around the room, still scowling. He surveyed the paintings and paused before a shelf full of crystal sculptures of sleek animals. He rested his hand on the head of a happy dolphin, gave it a pat, then turned back to me.

"See all dis stuff, Bubba? The rug, the art, all my possessions? They don't mean shit to me."

I said nothing, but my eyebrows rose.

"No, I mean it. I could walk away from here right now, and forget any of dis shit ever existed. That's what I did when I left N'Awlins. There was some trouble with the law, and I just walked away. My bidness, my house, the people I knew—poof!—gone."

"And you don't miss it?" My life was so firmly embedded, I couldn't move across town, much less vanish into another city a thousand miles away.

Sultan shook his head slowly. "No emotional attachments, Bubba. None. Dat's the only way to make it in de world. I care about two things: control and respect. When somethin's outta control, I fix it or I shut it down."

"But what about Lorrie Quintana? You're upset she was killed. There's no emotional attachment there?"

"Dat's where the respect comes in, Bubba. I'm mad because somebody's takin' me too lightly."

"That's all this is about, respect? You don't care about these girls?"

Sultan's face went icy and he stared at me until I squirmed. "You ask too many goddamn questions, Bubba."

I shrugged, looked away. I could feel his eyes on me, but he finally got tired of it and sighed and flopped back onto the sofa.

"So, Rosie Corona's involved in dis, eh?"

"I never said—"

"Dat bitch. She's been plaguin' me for years."

"I don't think she has anything to do with the killings," I said quickly. "I just went to see if she had any ideas about who's doing them."

"And what'd she say?"

"I told you. She ran me off with a gun and that big dog. I didn't get anything from her except a hard time."

The thought of Baby set off twinges of pain in my back and ribs. I was still stiff as peanut brittle from that fall.

"You keep after her. I think she's in it deep."

"But why?" I heard Felicia's words coming out of my own mouth. "What's the motivation? She's trying to help these hookers, not kill them."

Sultan sat up straighter, glared at me like I was an idiot. "You believe dat? You believe what you heard about SCORE?"

His tone made me pause. "Sure. Why not?"

"'Cause it's gatorshit, Bubba. SCORE's a cover. Rosie Corona's after de bidness along de Cruise. She don't give two shits about de other hookers."

"But the newspapers said—"

"Fuck dat, Bubba. You can't believe what you read in de papers."

I wondered what Felicia would say to that. It wouldn't be pretty. The thought of her led me to try another angle with Sultan Sweeney.

"I was thinking some of these religious types might be involved. You know, the ones who've been holding the rallies? Maybe one of them flipped out and started killing the girls."

Sultan looked me over coldly. "Come on, Bubba. Dat de best you can do?"

I tried to look shamefaced. Sultan leaned toward me, pointed a manicured finger my way.

"Dis ain't about religion, Bubba. It's bidness."

I left Sultan Sweeney's house still in his employ, but no clearer on what to do next. Sultan didn't seem to have any leads to offer, but there was no doubt he wanted me to find some, damned quick.

I needed a drink, and I wasn't going to find one in Ridgecrest. I drifted up Carlisle to Central, turned toward home.

I slowed as I passed the Paradise Motel. The cops

were gone. Nothing moved behind the rain-stained curtains in Lorrie Quintana's windows.

Down the sidewalk, at the corner, a woman stood hip-cocked in hot pants, waiting on a trick. As I passed her I recognized the bleached blonde who'd been weeping over Lorrie Quintana's passing an hour ago. She looked gaunt and red-eyed, but her makeup had been fixed and there was no question she was working.

Emotions are like that game kids play, slapping their fists into paper, scissors, rock. Fear is stronger than grief. The craving for a fix is stronger than any. She probably needed one after seeing her friend's head smashed like a melon that fell off the truck. I wondered whether she worked for Sultan Sweeney.

A horn blared behind me, awakening me to the fact the Chevy had slowed to a crawl. I looked in the mirror at a jacked-up purple van. The mustachioed driver was leaning over his steering wheel, shaking a finger at me while his jaws flapped. I tapped the brake just enough to make red lights flare in his face, and he stomped his brakes and tires squealed and the van fishtailed. I floored the accelerator and sped off. Fucker. Mess with me while I'm thinking. My revolver nudged me in the kidney. Moments like these are why people shouldn't carry guns in their cars.

Once home, I slipped into the cool of my room, set the gun on the dresser, made myself a drink. My head had a steady throb, like a clock ticking off the minutes until the next hooker would be killed. And, so far at least, there wasn't a damned thing I could do to stop it.

14

I brooded in my easy chair for a while, but Sultan Sweeney's impatience and that clock ticking in my head finally forced me to my feet. I turned on all the lights and fixed a quick bite and a cup of instant coffee. I had to get up and get moving. Like Mama used to say, nobody ever drowned in his own sweat.

I wanted to hit the Cruise, see if I could pick up any leads on Lorrie Quintana, but I still had a few hours until dark. I decided to work on Alice Burden's case for a while, maybe take my mind off the murders. I needed to circulate among the city's pawnshops with photos of the kewpie dolls. Now was as good a time as any.

Pawnbrokers will tell you they don't want stolen goods. If they give a thief pawn money, and the cops stumble across the item in their stores, it's not only heat on them, but they lose both the money and the item. Plus, the cops have a system where the pawnbrokers have to record everything they buy and give weekly lists to the police. The cops run the serial numbers through a computer to see if they match with any from burglary takes around the city.

Of course, not everything comes with a serial number. And if the goods are worth enough, the pawnbroker might be tempted to omit them from his records. No way the cops could tell. Some of these pawnshops have bigger inventories than Sears. Easy enough to hide something in there.

Even if a pawnbroker hadn't bought the kewpie dolls, one of them might've been offered the collection, might've seen it. The police computer system has been working this way for years, but burglars regularly get caught taking goods to pawnshops. Thieves aren't very smart. Otherwise, they'd be lawyers.

If pawnbrokers were smarter, it seemed, they'd all be comedians. I had to listen to a lot of jokes about the kewpie dolls as I visited one hock shop after another. The signs on the pawnshops should be a tipoff. They've got names like Loan Ranger and The Happy Hocker and Hock It to Me. Guess you should expect a Vegas act, which was what I got. Gruff, gold-draped pawnbrokers snorting as I showed them the photographs, making cracks about blow-up sex dolls and little boys who play with dolls and private eyes who'll take any kind of case.

To these guys, the only valuable goods are jewelry and electronics and musical instruments and tools. Things people look for secondhand. An oddity like a kewpie doll could sit on the shelf a long time.

I took the abuse at each shop, listened to the pawnbrokers make wisecracks out of the sides of their mouths, usually to some flunky kept around just so they'd have a straight man. At each place, I gave the broker one of my business cards, asked him to call me if anyone tried to pawn the dolls, and got the hell out.

Outside one shop, I nearly crashed into Pirate, an East Central burglar who carried a large wooden stereo speaker under either arm. Pirate is a lean, bearded, hook-nosed biker who wears a scarf tight over his head all the time. His muscular arms are decorated with tattoos of women and ships and, as a nod to his nickname, a black flag bearing the Jolly Roger.

"Hey, Pirate, how you doing?"

"Whatcha know, Bubba?"

Pirate was intent on getting past me and into the pawnshop with the speakers, which he'd probably lifted somewhere and wanted to unload before the computers got humming on Monday morning. The speakers looked heavy.

"Hey, Pirate," I said quickly. "You heard anything about somebody trying to unload a doll collection?"

"Dolls? You mean like kids play with?"

"Sort of. Kewpie dolls."

"Naw, man, I don't know nothing about no dolls. Where could you fence 'em?"

"I was just asking myself that question."

"You might ask Bobby Hidalgo. I seen his car parked in front of Sideshow's place a few minutes ago."

I thanked Pirate and got out of his way so he could lug his booty into the shop.

It was less than a mile over to Sideshow Barnes's Central Avenue Tattoo Emporium. I jingled through the front door, looking for Bobby Hidalgo.

The walls of the place were covered with sketches of tattoo possibilities, from Snoopy to Sinbad, voluptuous women to souped-up cars, roses to racehorses. The thought of having someone punch such a design into my skin made me edgy.

Until recently, when rock stars began making tattoos popular again, most guys got them when they were in prison or in the military. Like it takes the collective posturing of several hundred womenless men to make anybody think he's tough enough for The Needle. Bobby Hidalgo, while probably Albuquerque's most successful fence, had never done time in the slam or a tour in the Army. In the world he inhabits, tattoos equate with tough, and that's good enough for Bobby to want several.

Sideshow Barnes squeezed through a doorway at the back of the shop. Sideshow is a wide giant of a man given to biker chic—a beard, a braid down his back, black leather clothing, and thick fists covered with rings shaped like silver skulls and screaming eagles. His body makes a broad canvas, decorated with a 3-D horror movie's worth of snarling tigers and screeching dragons. Sideshow learned tattooing when he worked in a carnival, mostly by watching somebody use the needle on his own body.

Today, Sideshow wore a leather vest with no shirt, showing off his collection of painful paintings. He slapped me on the back, happy to see me.

"Come on back," he said. "I'm in the middle of someone."

I followed Sideshow into the airless little booth where he creates his art. Bobby Hidalgo sat on a stool with his shirt off, leaning forward with his elbows on a padded table. He had a thin cigar clamped in his teeth and sweat on his high forehead. An open bottle of tequila stood at his elbow.

Sideshow squeezed past him and sat on a taller stool, leaned over Bobby. A quick count showed this would be Bobby Hidalgo's seventh tattoo, joining the ranks of serpents, hula dancers, and panthers that already decorated his lean upper body.

"Getting a tattoo, huh?" It was a stupid thing to say, but I was nervous.

"Who, me?" Bobby Hidalgo grinned around his cigar. "Naw, I'm just letting Sideshow play connect the dots on my back. He gets a kick out of it."

Sideshow grinned and said, "Hold still."

I flinched when he turned on the electric needle,

which sounded like a cross between a sewing machine and a low-speed dentist's drill. The tone changed when the needle struck skin, and the smile disappeared from Bobby's face. He looked away from me, didn't want me to see the pain in his eyes.

Despite my anxiety, I found myself edging around, trying to get a quick look at what design Sideshow was inking into his skin. They hadn't been at it long. Sideshow had only a general shape, what looked like it might be a woman wearing a hat, near Bobby's shoulder blade. Blood had seeped to the surface and the skin looked red and inflamed already.

"What're you getting?"

Bobby answered through clenched teeth. "Mother Teresa."

"Really?"

"Yeah, a gift for my mother. She's crazy about that dame."

If Mother Teresa only knew she soon would be going around on Bobby Hidalgo's back . . .

"It's a tough one," Bobby added. "The woman has so many lines in her face."

"I offered to make her younger for you," Sideshow said without looking up from his work.

"Naw, it wouldn't be the same."

The sound of that needle was making me crazy. My feet kept trying to move toward the door on their own.

"What you gonna get?" Bobby asked.

"Nothing for me, thanks. I'm too big a sissy."

It was the right thing to say. Bobby smiled around his cigar, satisfied, like I'd said his dick was bigger than mine.

"Could do some nice work on you," Sideshow grunted. "Something small, not too flashy."

"No thanks. Really. I just want to talk to Bobby for a minute."

"So talk."

"You heard anything about somebody trying to fence some dolls, a collection?"

"Dolls?"

"Yeah, kewpie dolls, like you used to get at the carnival."

"I remember those dolls," Sideshow said.

"Somebody stole a doll collection?" Bobby thought it was ludicrous, too.

"Yeah. Apparently, it's worth some money. Enough for the client to hire me to find them."

"What the hell would somebody want with dolls?"

"Who knows? Why do people collect baseball cards? You name it, some jackass will want to collect it."

Bobby smiled. This was a truth with which he was familiar. Some people collect tattoos.

"Well, nobody's come to me," he said. "Probably know I'd kick his ass if he showed up at my place with a bunch of dolls."

I didn't think Bobby Hidalgo was much of an ass-kicker himself, but he had plenty of people willing to do it for him.

"If anybody does, give me a call," I said, and placed one of my cards by his elbow. "I need all the help I can get."

Bobby gave me a wink that was as good as a nod, and I started backing out of there.

"Now, gentlemen, if you'll excuse me, I've got to go. The sound of that needle is giving me the jitters."

They both grinned at me, and then I let my feet take over and hurried for the door.

Even outside, I could hear the needle squeal.

15

The Cruise on Saturday night is something to see. Hookers of every age, race, and gender sashaying up and down the neon-lit sidewalks. Dark shapes in cars pulling over for quick parleys on services and rates. Jeeploads of testosterone-wild frat boys swilling beer and hooting. Freaks striding along on their own agendas, twitching and muttering to themselves. Even the portions of Central Avenue reclaimed by the yuppies were hopping, with their bars spilling over and fat cats bravely dining al fresco, making easy drive-by targets under their table umbrellas.

Patrol cars flashed at one intersection, and my heart fluttered. But it was just a wreck that slowed traffic while everyone rubbernecked. A Range Rover had creamed a Harley, spewing bits of chrome and glass all over the street. No sign of the biker—an ambulance had probably hauled him off—but a guy in a polo shirt wrung his hands while he talked to the cops, as if he feared the biker would be back to settle with him.

I drove the entire strip once, trying to get a feel for it. The Cruise seemed tense, stiff, not the rollicking circus of sex and drugs I'd come to expect. I told myself it might just be me, transferring my own tension to the street scene.

On my second pass along the Cruise, I spotted Smiling Earl's dark-windowed Lincoln outside a fried chicken joint. I made the block and parked beside him.

The driver's window hummed down and Earl's man, Otis, glared out at me, his face as black and belligerent as a gorilla's.

"Earl around?" I called to him.

"Who wants to know?"

"Aw, come on, Otis, you know me. Bubba Mabry. We go back years."

"Oh, that you, Mabry? You white folks all look alike to me."

"Cute."

Otis didn't smile. Just stared with yellow eyes until I fidgeted.

"So is Earl inside?"

"He be out in a second."

I had time to get out of my car and lean against the trunk before Smiling Earl appeared in the brightly lit parking lot, carrying three boxes of chicken that smelled like Mama's kitchen.

They call him Smiling Earl because of a scar that runs from the corner of his mouth up to his left ear. The scar had healed funny, knotty and twisted, the color of a Band-Aid. Everybody said Earl had been integrated. But they didn't say it to his face. The cops are still finding pieces of the pimp who slashed Earl, and that happened years ago.

Earl was self-conscious about the scar, and he had a habit of turning away as he spoke so you couldn't stare at it. Of course, that just made the urge to stare more unbearable, and you'd find yourself edging around for a look, and Earl would turn farther, until the two of

you would end up whirling around, dancing a taran-
tella. It was exhausting talking to Earl.

"Fried chicken?" I jeered across the lot to him.
"Ain't that a little cliché, Earl?"

Earl said nothing until he could set the boxes down
on the fender of the big black Lincoln Town Car, and
in the passing seconds, I feared my joke had set wrong
with him. Then he turned toward me, grabbed his
crotch, and said, "Cliché this."

I grinned. "How you doing, Earl?"

"Okay, Bubba, better'n some, worse'n others."

He looked like he was doing all right, in his shiny
gray suit and matching wide-brimmed hat. Earl's a
small man, and he makes up for it some with padded
shoulders and high-heeled shoes.

"You got a minute?"

"Sure, Bubba. Otis! Get out here and get this
chicken. And don't you get into it 'fore I get back."

Earl walked me across the parking lot to the shadow
of the building, bitching all the while about how you
had to watch the idiot teenagers who worked there or
they'd give you all wings and backs. I could imagine
some freckle-faced kid reacting to Smiling Earl's
demands. Earl probably didn't even have to pay.

Earl stopped, turned to one side so I couldn't see his
scar, watched me out of the corner of his eye.

"So what's shakin', Bubba?"

I told him I was investigating the murders, carefully
skirting who'd hired me. I didn't want Earl seeing me
as the competition.

"Shit, man, good luck. Everybody been on the
lookout for the bastard's been offin' those girls, but
nobody's turned him up. Man's ruinin' our business."

"Looks like you're doing all right to me, Earl."

"Livin' off my investments, man. I need some fresh
money, and there ain't much of it coming my way
since people been getting killed down here."

"The johns staying away?"

"That, and my girls all hopped up about it. They don't want to get out there and work. Me and Otis been havin' to stay after they asses."

I didn't want to know what it took to get the girls to hit the streets, though I couldn't imagine Earl having much trouble with it. This scary little scarred man and his even scarier sidekick probably could get *me* turning tricks if they glared at me hard enough. Not that they'd make any money that way.

"I was thinking maybe it's some psycho been doing the killings," I said. "You got any leads along those lines?"

Earl turned some more to keep the scar out of sight. I tried not to stare.

"Bubba, if I knew who was doin' it, he'd already be dead."

"Really? But it's not your girls getting hit."

"Don' matter. I told you, mothafucka ruining our business. Whether it's my girls or Sultan Sweeney's, he can't just kill 'em. Shit, man, Sultan gonna run out of girls eventually. Then that freak gonna have to turn to somebody else."

"What about that, Earl? Why does he only hit Sultan's girls?"

He stroked his little goatee, mulling it over.

"Can't say, Bubba. Maybe just lucky for the rest of us. Maybe somebody's trying to run Sultan out of business."

"Could Sultan be doing them himself?"

Earl looked up at me from under his hat brim. "That what you think?"

"I don't know, Earl. That's why I'm asking you."

"Well, I tell you, I wouldn't cross that street to piss on Sultan Sweeney, that's how much I think of him. But it ain't him killin' those girls. Why would he wipe out his own harem?"

I nodded to show he had a point. "What about Rosie Corona? Think she could have anything to do with it?"

The one eye I could see widened. "That bitch? Why you think she's involved?"

"I don't know. I just heard some things."

"You been listenin' to the wrong people, Bubba. Rosie Corona's a pain in the ass, but she's no killer."

"She hates Sultan."

"Lotta people do."

Earl glanced back toward the Lincoln, and I could tell he was thinking about his chicken getting cold. I talked faster.

"Between some asshole killing the girls, and Rosie Corona trying to get the rest of them off the street, I'd think you have a problem."

Earl smiled, turned just enough that the scar flashed at me.

"They's always mo' girls, Bubba."

I turned Earl loose to go eat his supper. Standing there smelling that hot grease so long, I decided I had to have some of that chicken myself. I entered the fluorescent glare, ordered a SnakPak, paid for it with some of Sultan Sweeney's money, and carried the hot box out to my car. Smiling Earl's car was gone. I cranked up the Chevy and was moving down Central before I opened the box of chicken. Wings and backs.

I wandered the Cruise for half an hour before I spotted one of Sultan Sweeney's girls. She went by the name of Melody, and she'd been playing tunes along Central for years. I pulled the Chevy to the curb and leaned across to her.

"Hi there, big boy," she said. "You looking for a date?"

"Hello, Melody. You're working for Sultan Sweeney now, right?"

Terror flashed on her face, and she backed away

from the car. I guess being connected to Sultan wasn't the safest thing these days.

"Hey, Melody, come on," I called to her. "You know me. Bubba Mabry. I'm working for Sultan, too."

She bent over, squinted into the Chevy's interior. I flicked on the inside light so she could see I wasn't the killer.

"What do you mean, you're working for Sultan?"

"I'm trying to find whoever's been killing his girls."

I watched her relax. She was wearing a black tube top over smallish breasts, and tight gray sweatpants cut off at the knees. Her brown hair spilled around her face, shadowing her expression.

"What do you want from me?"

"I thought maybe you could give me some tips. Tell me what you know about it."

"I don't know nothing, except that I'm scared to death."

"Come on, climb in. We'll just talk for a few minutes."

She glanced up and down the street, looking for a john with a better offer. Then she shrugged and opened the door. She sat close to the door, keeping an eye on me, like she was ready to bail out at the first sign I was the psycho killer.

I pulled back into the slow traffic, and we poked along, me watching the road, Melody watching me.

"My feet hurt," she said. "Mind if I take off my shoes?"

I shook my head, and she wrenched the high heels off her feet and wiggled her toes. I noted she kept the shoes in her hands, ready to bury the spikes in my head if I made a wrong move. Smart girl.

"I remember you now," she said. "You're that guy who thought he saw Elvis Presley."

I flinched at the mention of his name.

"Yeah, well, that was a long time ago."

"Not so long. What, a year ago?"

"Something like that." My tone said change the subject, and she obliged.

"You heard what happened to Lorrie?" she asked.

"I was there when the cops wheeled her away."

"She's number four. Sultan has fewer girls all the time, and that puts pressure on the rest of us."

"How many are left?"

"I don't know exactly. Three or four. Sultan doesn't talk to us about such things."

"Yeah, but you talk to each other."

"Some." Suspicious now, wondering where I was headed.

"Have any of the girls said anything about somebody who acted angry or violent?"

"You mean like a dissatisfied customer?"

"Yeah. Or, uh, some guy who slapped them around or, you know, got kinky."

She pressed her lips together, like she had me sized up.

"You mean like the old guy who wanted to spank me with a big pink rubber dick?"

"Well, not exactly—"

"Or the cop who tried to poke his nightstick up my ass?"

"No, what I meant was—"

"Or the guy who tied me up in bed, then pierced my ears?"

"Your ears?"

She tossed back her hair, tapped a dangling earring with her finger.

"Did a good job of it, too. But it hurt like hell."

"Jesus—"

"You know, mister, I usually get paid to talk dirty."

"Lord, Melody, that's not what I wanted. I thought

you might have some idea who was killing people. That's all."

"What do you want me to say? 'I know some freak who likes to rape women, then bash in their heads? Maybe he's your killer?' Come on. It's never that simple. Just because a guy's kinky, or even into pain, doesn't mean he's out to kill someone. Everybody's got their little quirks."

"Murder is more than a quirk."

"You're telling me? Every time I get in a car with somebody, he could turn out to be the one who finishes it for me."

She paused, stared out at the passing storefronts.

"And then every night I get to answer my door and give half my hard-earned money to Sultan Sweeney."

"How come? You've been around awhile, Melody. Why don't you free-lance?"

"Because I'm more scared of Sultan than of all the kinky losers you could round up along the Cruise."

I said nothing, swallowed hard against a lump in my throat.

"If you're working for Sultan, you should be scared, too."

"Why's that?"

She shot me a look like she couldn't believe I hadn't already figured it out.

"If somebody's killing all the girls who work for Sultan, eventually he'll get to me," she said, her voice low and certain. "And if he's killing everybody who works for Sultan, eventually he'll get to you."

I tried to summon up some bravado. "Not if I find him first."

"If you find him first, that'll probably just move you up the list. No offense, mister, but better you than me."

"Thanks."

She smiled, but weariness showed in her eyes.

"Here's another what-if," she said. "Maybe the cops will bring heat down on Sultan, and he'll need a fall guy. You seem to fit the bill."

"What you're saying is, maybe Sultan's killing his own girls."

She shrugged her thin shoulders. "Who knows? I believe he's capable of anything."

We said nothing for a while. Blue streetlight glare rippled over us in the car.

"Look," she said finally, "if you want a second opinion, turn right at the next street. Talk to Side Street Sally."

"Side Street Sally?"

"Yeah, she's new. Still working the side streets because she's afraid someone she knows will see her along Central. She'll get over it."

I made the turn and, sure enough, there stood a nervous hooker, close to a utility pole, like she wasn't advertising anything.

Melody slipped her shoes back on as the car came to a halt.

"Better let me talk to her first," she said.

I leaned across the car and smiled and tried to look unthreatening while Melody explained what I wanted. Sally kept cutting her eyes toward me. She wore a tight little dress with a zipper up the front and black heels with lace-trimmed socks. She was maybe twenty years old, looked younger. Looked scared.

When Melody finished, Sally closed her eyes and sighed. Then she nodded silently and got in the car. I gave Melody a little wave, but she'd already turned away toward the bright lights of Central Avenue.

"Melody says you're a private eye."

"That's right."

"And you're working for Sultan?"

"Yeah. He hired me to find out who killed your co-workers."

"Don't call them that. I don't think of them as my co-workers."

I thought about what Melody had said: She'll get over it.

"So, Melody tells me you're new to the 'life.'"

"It's just a temporary thing." There was an edge to her voice. "Just until Sultan can get out of the business."

"Is that so? Sultan's going to quit?"

"Yes. And then we're going to be married."

I tried not to roll my eyes. "He told you that, huh?"

"Mm-hmm. It's going to be wonderful."

"That's funny. He didn't say anything to me about it."

"Well, he's keeping it a secret for now. If we let it out, the other girls wouldn't work for him anymore. He's trying to save up enough money for us to get a new start."

I wondered whether Sultan used this ploy with all the girls, or just the ones young enough to believe it.

"So you don't think he has anything to do with his girls getting killed?"

I glanced over in time to see her go wide-eyed at the thought, but she quickly convinced herself and said, "Sultan wouldn't do a thing like that. He's the sweetest man I've ever met."

I wondered about the other men in her life. Probably an abusive father. A string of boyfriends who got what they wanted, then moved on. Maybe even a young husband who'd slapped her around. It must've been a bad run of louts and freaks to make that cold snake Sweeney look sweet to her.

"So you don't have any idea who might be the killer?"

"For all I know, it's you. It could be anyone."

"Well, it's not me. But that's all I can say for certain. Why do you keep doing it if you're so scared?"

Her eyes narrowed to slits, like I wouldn't understand no matter what she said.

"I'm careful."

"You'd better be."

She opened her door. "If you see Sultan," she said, "tell him I'm thinking about him."

She closed the door and walked away without looking back.

Talking to Sultan's girls gave me an itchy feeling, the same twitch I get when I find a corpse. Deena's lithe young body and twisted neck flashed through my mind, and I tried to push it away. Melody was right. It could be just a matter of time before the killer struck them all. And time was running out. The killings were getting more frequent. Only five days between the last two, where the killer had been waiting weeks before.

The Cruise had emptied out, one of those lulls when all the hookers have found johns and everybody's hunkered down in motel rooms. I drove aimlessly for a while, then got one more idea.

I drove toward the mountains until I reached the red light at Morningside Drive, then made the block a couple of times, waiting for the drag queens to appear from the shadows.

My trolling worked the third time I rounded the block, and a six-foot black in spike heels and an elaborate wig waited at the curb. I let the Chevy roll to a stop.

"Hey, pretty lady, you got a minute?"

The queen bent over, flashing me a smile, and I popped on the interior light so he could see it was me.

"Bubba Mabry! You old rascal!"

"Hello, Willis."

"It's Wilhemina tonight, Bubba."

"Excuse me, madam." That made him smile. "I need to talk. Want to go for a spin around the block?"

Willis turned and held up a finger to someone in the shadows of the alley, signaling he'd be right back. Then he climbed into the car, his tight purple skirt crawling up high on his shaved thighs. He wore magenta lipstick and eye shadow painted all the way out to his thin brows.

"I don't know how you do it."

"Do what?"

"Pluck your eyebrows like that. Doesn't it hurt?"

Willis puckered his lips at me. "Beauty hurts, Bubba. But it's worth it."

Now it was my turn to smile.

I didn't know many of the drag queens anymore. Once you made it clear you weren't interested in a tumble, most didn't waste their time on you. But I'd known Willis for years, since he was a strapping teen making his movie money by dealing blow jobs along Central. I'd even stepped in once when a couple of rednecks were roughing him up. Between the two of us, we'd made a good night's work of kicking the shit out of them. Willis never forgot.

Over the years, Willis had gone more and more feminine. He probably didn't own a pair of pants anymore. I didn't know if it was hormones, like so many of the queens take, or just an attitude he'd adopted. Some things you don't ask.

"I heard about Felix," I said. The drag queens are a close-knit group. Willis would've known him.

"Oh, wasn't that terrible?" Willis's voice rose. "That poor girl, she didn't have a chance. And to get cut up like that. Brrr."

"Yeah, the cops think the same freak has been killing girls working for Sultan Sweeney. You heard about that?"

"We've all heard, Bubba. In case you haven't noticed, things are tense around here. They've even got an old gal like me anxious. Nothing in this purse but condoms and a straight razor."

"You're ready for him, huh?"

"As ready as a girl can be. I got to keep working, else I end up like a lot of the others, staying home watching soap operas and getting fat while the cops hunt him down."

"People that scared?"

"You better believe it. Those preachers getting all red in the face trying to shut down the Cruise, but these murders may do the job for them."

"Has anyone been talking about who might be doing it? Have you heard anything strange?"

Willis grinned lasciviously. "Bubba, when you work my corner, just 'bout everything you hear is something strange."

"True."

"You want to know what I think?"

"That's why we're talking."

"I think Felix surprised somebody. He was so young and pink and hairless that a lot of straight guys thought he was for real. He'd get them back to his room, get some booze in them, then, surprise! He's got a dick where his pussy should be."

I thought, Not anymore.

"Some men aren't very flexible," Willis concluded. "They take that the wrong way."

"But that wouldn't explain Sultan Sweeney's girls getting killed."

Willis shrugged. "You never know down here. All I know is I expect to die a quiet death of AIDS one of these days, and I don't want somebody cutting it short for me."

"Don't joke about that."

"Why not, Bubba? You got to laugh. You think I

could keep turning out here in these high heels every night if I didn't have a sense of humor?"

I stopped the car at Willis's corner.

"It was good to see you again, Bubba. Don't be a stranger."

He blew me a kiss, then he was gone, back into the shadows.

I drove away, thinking about what he'd said about Felix. I knew what it was like to be surprised. Once, when I was a young burrhead at Kirtland Air Force Base, I'd met a blonde in a dark bar and gone home with her, drunk and anticipatory. It wasn't until we got to her room, and the light was better, that I noticed the slightest five o'clock shadow under the thick makeup. I had no urge to pummel the guy. I just wanted out of there.

The queen had pleaded with me to stay, to spend the night, saying, "A mouth is a mouth, no matter whose it is," an argument that failed to persuade me. Luckily, I was just sober enough to make my way to the door.

Even though nothing had happened, I'm still edgy whenever I think how close it had been. Another file in the drawer marked "Gullibility." Sometimes it seems that drawer must be full.

The memories left me depressed, and I went on home to drink and think and sleep.

My message machine blinked at me as I came in the door, and I hit the tape and heard Felicia's voice inviting me to Sunday brunch at her place, since our Saturday visit had been cut short when I zoomed off to see Dudley. That seemed like weeks ago.

I dialed her number, and it rang four times and then her machine came on the line. It was late, but she must've still been at the office. I pictured her perched over her keyboard, pounding out tomorrow's news, puffing smoke like a locomotive. This was the way we communicated these days, since she'd gone to work at the *Gazette*. Have your machine call my machine. We'll do lunch.

I left a message that I'd be there. Then I turned off the ringer on my phone. I'd talked to enough people for one night.

16

I knew Felicia had more than breakfast on her mind when she opened the door. The first thing to hit me was a whiff of perfume rather than the usual blast of stale cigarette smoke. Felicia was wearing lipstick—again, not the usual—and her hair was brushed shiny. She wore the usual floor-length blue bathrobe, but something black and lacy and tantalizing peeked from the V the robe made over her breasts. My insides fluttered in anticipation. In short, she was loaded for bear, and I was feeling grizzly.

The only sign she'd been working in the kitchen was a smudge of something like wallpaper paste on her nose where she'd pushed up her eyeglasses.

I followed her to the kitchen, which wasn't the wreck it usually is when she's cooking. We were having something simple, she told me, bagels and lox. Still, empty cartons and wrappers were scattered on the counter, one of them leaking salmon juice, along with an arsenal of knives, each glued to the Formica with a smear of cream cheese.

She'd set the table, even had a single daisy in a vase

in the center. The coffee was hot and the food looked good and Felicia had a glitter in her eye like she might rake it all on the floor and throw me over the table any second. Like in the movies, where people make love everywhere but in bed. It always makes my joints ache to see people doing it on a tabletop or a hardwood floor. But the way I felt as I looked at her, I was willing to give it a try.

Without breaking eye contact, she picked up her loaded-down bagel and took a big bite. Even that looked sexy, and when she licked her lips, whew. But Felicia wasn't ready to skip the rest of the meal and dash for the bedroom. She wanted something first.

"So what did Dudley say?"

That broke the spell. I sighed with longing and gazed at my plate. Maybe I could transfer my lust to eating.

"He said he'd sue me if I ever took his name in vain again."

Felicia grinned, brushed her hair back with her wrist.

"Bubba! What did you say to him?"

"Nothing, really. I just suggested someone he knows might be offing those hookers."

"Someone he knows?"

"You know, someone he knows well. Like the guy he sees when he's shaving every morning."

Felicia laughed and her cheeks flushed and the sparkle in her eyes made it worth all the abuse I'd taken from Dudley.

Naturally, she demanded a blow-by-blow description of my conversation with the city councilman. I told her what Alice Burden had said about Dudley's high school exploits. Then I told her about visiting Jericho, how I'd hinted his boy Dudley might be the one.

"Oh, Bubba, you didn't!"

"Well, he didn't seem to know. I hate for anybody to be missing the latest gossip. Especially a preacher."

Felicia was halfway through her food, chewing excitedly. "This explains a lot," she said. "I tried to call Dudley and Jericho all day yesterday, and could never raise either of them."

"What, you think they were together talking about me?" The alarming thought of a lawsuit clanged in my head.

"Maybe. Or maybe Jericho told Marilyn Dudley what you said. That would've stirred up a hornet's nest."

"Dudley's wife? Why would he tell her?"

"What if I told you I thought something was going on between Jericho and Marilyn Dudley?"

"Something going on? You mean like an affair?"

That was hard to picture. That skinny, stiff woman and that scrawny little preacher humping away somewhere. They were both so bony, they'd cut themselves on each other. Plus, they were so *fervent*. Jericho, at least, seemed a hard-core believer, someone who felt God personally looked over his shoulder all the time, watched his every move, and it was important to keep the Big Guy happy. I couldn't imagine Jericho grunting "Sweet Jesus!" while he pelvisized someone, or going down on his knees for anything but prayer.

"Maybe not an affair," Felicia said. "Maybe not even a flirtation. But I can tell you this much, Marilyn Dudley is much closer to Reverend Jericho than her husband is."

"That's not much to go on."

"I wasn't going anywhere with it. It's just something I've wondered about. It might be the chink in their armor."

Felicia had that ardent glow that comes when she's hot on somebody's trail, and that was not the ardor I had in mind. It was time to change the subject.

"This food sure is good."

"Thanks. You know, I've been suspicious of Jericho from the start. Ever since I heard that ridiculous name of his and tracked down his real name."

"His real name?"

"Jeckle."

"You mean like Doctor Jekyll?"

"No, like Heckle and Jeckle, those crows on the cartoons."

I didn't remember any crows from my cornflake Saturday mornings in front of the tube, but I tried not to get steered away again.

"Lots of people change their names. Nothing wrong with that."

"But a preacher? It doesn't seem . . . honest."

"Happens all the time."

"Really?"

"Sure. Oral Roberts's real name is Anal. I thought everybody knew that."

Felicia set down her bagel. "You're soooo funny."

"I can't help myself. I've got anatomy on my mind."

I waggled my eyebrows at her, and she finally let go a laugh. I felt sure we were headed for the bedroom now, that she wouldn't send me chasing on another errand. But she kept talking.

"There's another protest rally tonight. Why don't you come out to see it? I've got to be there anyway. We can watch these three, and you can tell me there's not something fishy there. Jericho's always sniffing around Marilyn, looking after her like she's more than his top disciple. Or at least like he wants her to be more. And Dudley seems a little removed, you know? Like he's going through the motions on the whole crusade, and hasn't even noticed Marilyn's spending all her time with Jericho."

The thought of attending another of those rallies made me lose my appetite, but I feared I'd lose more than that if I didn't go along with her, so I said, "Sure, I'll be there."

"With the election coming up, things are getting tense anyway," she said. "They'll probably be even more tense now that you've noodled them a little."

It occurred to me Quentin Dudley would not be pleased if he spotted me in the crowd.

"Well, I'm pretty tense myself."

"Really?" She gave her hair a little toss and smiled. "How about if we relieve your tension in the other room?"

"I thought you'd never ask."

Watching me, smiling, she rose from the table. I tossed my napkin across to her.

"But first, wipe the cream cheese off your nose. Okay?"

17

I emerged from Felicia's apartment two hours later, feeling relaxed and bubbly. I'd left her sitting up in bed with her glasses on, promising she'd rise soon and get ready for work. She said she felt too wonderful to get up right away. I practically tap-danced down the stairs from her apartment.

Sex with someone you love is the best. As tormented and twisted as our relationship sometimes seemed, I couldn't deny my feelings for Felicia. And, despite her misgivings, she felt the same way about me. Moments like these, when love and satisfaction swelled inside my chest like a happy balloon, reminded me why we stuck with it.

I tooled along in the Chevy, whistling snatches of unrecognizable songs into the warm air pouring through the windows. It was one of those perfect spring days when the cloudless skies reach all the way to heaven and the winds are calm and the sun warms your skin without making you sweat. I felt pretty warm on the inside, too.

Which is why I was so surprised when I got to my place. I was at ease for once, and the last thing I expected was for someone to start yelling down my throat.

I'd just unlocked the door when Marilyn Dudley appeared at my side. She was still in her church clothes, a severe dark suit over a high-necked Victorian blouse, and she looked hot. Her face was red, and a dark tress had freed itself from her hairdo and was stuck to her forehead.

"Mr. Mabry, I presume."

I nodded.

"Inside."

As soon as the door closed behind her, I realized obeying was a mistake. She would've been less likely to get loud out on the sidewalk.

"How dare you!"

"Wha—"

"Who do you think you are?!"

"Now, don't—"

"How dare you spread rumors about my husband!"

"Ma'am, I—"

"He's the finest public servant this city has ever known! He's a good man, a Christian man, and a good husband. And you—" She looked around for the first time, and her face showed disgust. "—you live *here!*"

"Now, wait a minute—"

"I should've known," she said, her voice dripping. "I should've known someone like you was responsible. Someone on *Central* who's unnerved by the way we're bringing God down here."

"Look, I don't care what your religious—"

"You probably work for criminals and pimps."

This time I couldn't choke up any objection. Which was just as well, she wasn't slowing.

"I had to sit in that filthy parking lot for an hour, waiting for you. With those dirty men leering in at me, and women doing their laundry in their underwear. It's worse down here than I ever imagined."

"Then why don't you just hustle on back up to the Heights?"

She stabbed a finger under my nose, close enough that I felt the wind from it.

"Watch your mouth, buddy." This was a new tone for her, something left over from her days as boss of the schoolyard. It still worked, or at least it worked on me. I clammed up.

"Spreading rumors is a sin, mister." Exactly what Jericho had said. "No less a sin than what the pimps and prostitutes and the drug pushers do down here. God has put a black mark in His Book beside your name."

I thought, It'll have plenty of company.

"God is watching, you know. He knows everything that goes on down here, every sinful thought, every lustful temptation. He knows evil lives on Central Avenue. And He's no longer willing to ignore it. Look what's happened to those prostitutes."

"Wait a second. You mean God is responsible for the murders?"

Her face screwed up into an ugly mask and she spat at me, "I said zip it. I'm doing the talking here."

I took another step away from her. I couldn't go far, not without climbing over the bed. And that would seem cowardly.

"Who can say how God operates? But He's responsible for everything. Whoever's killing those women, God is allowing it."

Deena's twisted neck flashed into my mind. And Lorrie Quintana, her head as flat and pop-eyed as a goldfish's. And Felix the drag queen's impromptu surgery.

"No, ma'am, I don't think God was looking when those killings happened. Maybe Jesus tapped Him on the shoulder or something, but nobody could stand by—"

"Don't you blaspheme!" The finger was under my nose again. Her other arm still tightly clutched her big black handbag, and it occurred to me she could have a gun in there. Or a knife. Maybe God's wrath had arrived at my doorstep. I edged away some more. She followed.

"Don't take God lightly, Mr. Mabry. He's a vengeful God, a jealous God. He allows no others before Him. And He doesn't allow Sin to triumph."

"No, ma'am." Couldn't this just be over?

She turned from me, unclasped the purse and dug around in there. Now was my chance to jump her, before she could pull out the pistol, before she could wheel on me with the steak knife. I just stood there, frozen by religion, like I'd been caught taking from the collection plate.

She pulled a crumpled piece of white paper from the purse and turned to wave it at me.

"Do you know what this is?"

I shook my head. It wasn't a gun, and that was good enough for me.

"Reverend Jericho slipped me this note as he shook my hand on the way out of church this morning. Do you know what it says?"

More head shaking.

"It says you're spreading rumors about my husband. That you hinted he could have something to do with prostitutes. Can you imagine how mortified I was to get such a note at such a place?"

I felt like my head was going to shake off my neck.

"Is it true? Did you say that?"

"Not exactly—"

"Don't lie to me! Reverend Jericho is a servant of God. He wouldn't make up something like this."

She put the note back in her purse and closed the clasp with a satisfied snap. I waited for whatever would come next, but she seemed to be running out of gas.

"So what happens now?" I asked, not sure I wanted to hear the answer.

"What happens? You've violated the Commandments, and you don't know what happens? Damnation, that's what. An eternity of hellfire. Are you ready for that, mister?"

"I meant what happens now, right now. You can't just keep me cornered in my room all day."

"That's the least I'd like to do to you."

That murderous tone crept into her voice again. It scared me more than the hysteria.

"I'll tell you what I'm going to do." She jabbed me in the chest with her finger. "I'm going to go home and get down on my knees and pray that bad things happen to you. I'm going to ask God to render immediate judgment on your actions."

"You think God listens to those kind of prayers?"

"God listens to me. You wait and see. And the next time something bad happens to you, when you're in a car wreck or someone robs you or you get sick, think of me. Because I'll be responsible for it."

She turned and stalked out, slamming the door behind her.

I stood there a long time. Great, I thought, now God's going to be mad at me, too.

I shakily poured myself a drink, but someone pounded on my door before I could take a sip. I crept across the room and opened the door a crack, ready to slam it shut if Marilyn Dudley had come back for more.

Borkum and Bates stood grinning in at me, holding up their badges out of habit. Borkum put a thick hand on the door and leaned his weight against it, and I stepped back and let them in.

While I closed the door, Borkum moved to the

middle of the room. He unzipped his windbreaker so I could see his gun, put his badge in his shirt pocket, and hitched under his belly at his pants. His skinny partner skittered around the edges of the room like a rat, looking everything over, touching my stuff.

"So, Mabry, looks like you're associating with a better class of people." Borkum grinned at me with those wide lips. The way his eyes were, I couldn't tell if he was watching me or Norman. "Why's a city councilman's wife coming to see you?"

I had no immediate answer, wasn't about to repeat the Quentin Dudley rumors to these two gas bags. Norman paused in his rummaging and looked over his shoulder.

"Better answer him, Mabry," he said quietly, as if talking about an abusive spouse. "He's in a rotten mood today."

I could see that much for myself. Borkum's brow had creased over his floater eye, so that his forehead looked like a wadded paper bag, and the wide grin had disappeared.

"That's right," he said. "I hate working on Sundays. I don't care about overtime. I just want to be home in front of the TV. Instead, I'm out here talking to scum because the mayor wants to crack down on the Cruise. Christ, I hate elections."

I gathered I was the "scum" he was referring to, but I didn't take the bait. Borkum was looking for someone to tee off on, and I wasn't going to help him out this time.

"So what was Marilyn Dudley doing here, peckerhead?"

"She wanted some advice."

"Advice? From you?"

"She was trying to get some information on the Cruise. Guess she thought I was something of an expert in that area."

"You? An expert? That's a laugh. I wouldn't call somebody dumb enough to work for Sultan Sweeney an expert on anything."

I shrugged, said nothing.

"Don't you know what kind of lowlife you're dealing with? Sweeney is the lowest. He's beneath pond scum. He's bedrock."

Borkum wasn't about to get me defending Sultan Sweeney. Even if I'd had that inclination, it was clear from the way he was worked up that he'd need very little excuse to get rough. For once, I'd keep my mouth shut.

Borkum glared at me with his good eye; the floater didn't seem too interested, just wandered around the room.

"And I'm beginning to think you're bedrock scum, too, Mabry. At least Sultan Sweeney came by his criminal attitude honestly. You're just suffering from exposure."

He leaned toward me a few inches.

"Don't think you're tough, Mabry. You're not."

I tried to smile in his face, but I don't think it worked. Probably looked like I was passing a kidney stone.

"Nobody on the Cruise is tough as he thinks. They may come on like bad men, but I know what it takes to make 'em whimper."

The memory of his hard knee between my legs caused a stab of pain in my groin. Had I whimpered? Probably.

Expecting more of the same, I thought briefly of bolting for the door. I could probably make it through before Borkum could get his hands on me, but they'd run me down like hounds. And even if I got away, where could I hide where they couldn't find me?

Borkum stepped sideways, cutting off my line of

escape. I sighed, more with relief than disappointment. Now I had no decision to make; it was just a matter of riding out the shitstorm.

"Mayor wants to crack down on the Cruise, I'll tell him how to do it," Borkum said. "Wipe out the lowlifes, no questions asked. Make the world a better place. We could start by nuking all of Central Avenue, you included."

Bates suddenly spoke up, like he wanted to keep his partner from getting off on the mayor and the Sunday work schedule again. He'd probably heard enough of that for one day.

"What did Marilyn Dudley want to know?"

I'd been so busy keeping my mouth shut, I hadn't dreamed up an appropriate lie.

"She, um, she was worried that, uh, somebody in her movement might be in trouble."

"Her movement?"

"Yeah, you know, her and her husband and that Reverend Jericho. The folks who want to clean up Central."

"Yeah, yeah. So?"

"So she thinks somebody in the group might be connected to the murders. You know, some fanatic who might've taken God's will into his own hands."

"She say who she was talking about?"

"No. She seemed really upset, though. Like she might know something the rest of us don't."

That made Borkum glare harder at me. I wished he'd turn his head so his eyes would look the same direction. I kept feeling like I should look over my shoulder, see what he was staring at.

"I doubt there's much Marilyn Dudley could know about the Cruise that Bates and me don't know," he said.

I nodded, tried to look thoughtful.

"That's why she was looking for advice. She doesn't know shit about what goes on down here. She was asking me if I'd heard anything that might implicate any of her people."

I was warming to all this now. Not only did it seem I was talking my way out of trouble—after years of failed attempts—but I was giving Borkum and Bates new leads to check out, ones I'd already pretty much exhausted.

"And what did you tell her?" Bates demanded.

"Not much. It hadn't even occurred to me one of those Bible-thumpers might be the killer."

That was taking a chance. If they'd known about Marilyn Dudley coming to my room, maybe they'd been following me for days. How would I explain my visit to Jericho? But Borkum just grunted at my stupidity, and his partner pressed on.

"And that satisfied her? She looked pretty steamed when she went storming out of here."

"The lady wanted help. I wasn't able to give her any."

Borkum muttered something about what he'd like to give her, seeing as how she was partly responsible for him working on Sunday, but Norman ignored him. He stepped closer to me, looking me over like he was deciding where to bite me.

"Did you tell her you're a prime suspect yourself?"

"Me?" It was only one syllable, but my voice cracked.

"Yeah, you. You're working for Sultan Sweeney. Maybe he hired you to keep his girls in line. Every time there's a murder, you seem to be on the scene."

"Not every time."

"No, maybe not. Even you would be smart enough not to show up at every murder."

Now I was getting scared. I'd almost talked my way

out of this encounter, had begun to relax a little, to enjoy it. But the thought of getting hauled to the police station took all the fun out of it. Even if they had nothing on me—and it had to be nothing, right? I hadn't done anything—they could hold me long enough for a probing strip search and a delousing. Not the way I'd prefer to spend my Sunday.

"I didn't even know anything about these murders until that girl Deena turned up dead at this motel."

"You didn't?" Norman let his eyes go wide, playing with me. "But I thought you were the expert. You're the one city councilmen's wives come to see when they have a problem."

I hung my head.

Bates snorted and said to his partner, "Let's get out of here. I'm tired of looking at this loser."

My head tried to jerk up at the slur, but I kept it down. I'd had years of practice, hunkering down to avoid attention. Now was the time to put it to use.

Bates snatched open the door and strode into the sunshine. Borkum paused in front of me, and I watched his thick finger come into my field of vision, jab me once in the chest.

"We're watching you, baby doll. You'd better stay out of our way."

I locked the door after they left, thinking I'd be damned if I'd answer it again on this crazy Sunday. I peeked out the curtains until I saw their unmarked car pull away.

The drink I'd poured earlier stood empty on the counter. Bates must've tossed it off while Borkum was working me over. I got a clean glass out of the cabinet, poured a short one.

What is it with these Vice cops? Why do they care that I'm sniffing around in the murders? Homicides aren't their responsibility, no matter how much they see themselves as the Avengers of Central Avenue. Did they have something to hide? A thought I'd suppressed during Bates's questioning came swimming to the surface. They, too, had been at the scene of the Lorrie Quintana murder. Had they been at the others?

18

My head buzzed like a beehive. I'd felt wonderful for a little while, youthful and ardent and studly, but Marilyn Dudley and Borkum and Bates had brought the murder case crashing down on me again.

Determined to take the afternoon off, I flicked on the television. There was nothing on but baseball and golf and infomercials and some show about open-heart surgery, all of which I find equally exciting. I tried a paperback crime novel I'd been reading before Sultan Sweeney hired me, but I soon gave it up. I'd lost the thread, who was who in the story. Besides, the novel paled next to what I'd been going through lately in real life.

I took a fitful nap, and got up in time to wolf down a bologna sandwich before meeting Felicia at the sunset protest rally.

I thought about wearing a hat, a disguise of some sort, in case Quentin Dudley was there. But Felicia would probably laugh at me, and I hate hats. The way my hair is falling out, I may eventually learn to love them.

The rally was farther east than the earlier one, out past the state fairgrounds in the parking lot of a storefront church. Not as much traffic out here, but what pedestrians there were would be the type the fundamentalists were railing against. A few of the motels out here had been refurbished with new stucco and shrubs planted around, but the clientele hadn't changed.

The huge sign for a gay bar called Booze 'n' Cruise stood just down the block, and I thought it must be a bonus for the demonstrators to have some homosexuals to complain about, too.

I was on top of the rally before I saw the other protesters across the street and the handful of helmeted cops who'd shown up to keep the two groups separated. I took my foot off the gas and let the Chevy slow as I passed.

Across Central Avenue from the fundamentalists, the sidewalk was full of prostitutes. Hookers in hot pants, joy boys in tank tops, drag queens in false eyelashes and peignoirs, trying to look like Lana Turner. In the middle of them, dressed in jeans and a T-shirt, Rosie Corona led a chant.

"Slaves no more. You can SCORE! Slaves no more. You can SCORE!" Over and over.

The hookers waved homemade signs that said WE ARE BUSINESSWOMEN, WE HAVE A RIGHT TO MAKE A LIVING, STOP THE VIOLENCE ON THE CRUISE.

A TV cameraman stood in the median, squinting through his minicam lens at the chanting, laughing, bouncing hookers. Visions of ratings points dancing in his head. Cars crawled past, the motorists gawking at the TV camera as much as at the bright-feathered birds on the sidewalk. A few Bible-thumpers glared at the cameraman, but most were turned to the portable stage, where someone with a microphone was trying to outshout the hookers.

I swung the Chevy into the parking lot of the gay bar, which was nearly empty this time of day, and hurried on foot to the protest zone. I didn't want to miss any of this.

The crowd was the same fervent congregation as before, plus several dozen curious onlookers. I could see their cars parked haphazardly on the side streets, like they'd seen the protests, thought, What the hell, and pulled over to watch.

Once again I found the reporters clustered to one side, habitually distancing themselves. I squeezed into the pack and found Felicia on the far side, nearest the stage.

She smiled when she saw me, then looked at her watch to show me I was late, which I already knew.

I jerked my head toward the hookers across the street and said, "Looks like this story just moved to the front page."

Felicia shushed me, grabbed my arm, pulled me closer to her to get me out of someone's line of sight.

As usual, she'd wormed her way to the best vantage point. She had a full view of the stage—no sign of Dudley or his angry wife—and gaps in the crowd that lined up for a peek at the hookers. I could see Rosie Corona leading a new chant, her arms pumping above her head like a cheerleader's. She'd sure gotten her crowd worked up. Especially the drag queens, who flounced and falsettoed and vogued for the gawkers. It looked like a dance floor. During Mardi Gras.

> "Two, four, six, eight,
> Ain't no crime we perpetrate,
> Three, five, seven, nine,
> I turned the trick, the money's mine!"

On stage, one of Jericho's sidekicks tried to lead a hymn, but the distracted flock couldn't keep their minds on their bleating, and the hookers drowned them out.

> "We don't need no talk of sin,
> We need SCORE to help us win!"

I wondered how Rosie Corona had managed to get the hookers to turn out, much less rehearse chants. She must be quite the organizer. Most hookers have attention spans about as long as an orgasm.

I looked back at the stage to see Reverend Skip Jericho jump to his feet. Flustered over the muttered failure of the hymn, Jericho snatched the microphone away from the choir leader and boomed into it, "Welcome, brothers and sisters!"

That got a smattering of applause, got the church folk to wheel their heads around toward the stage.

"By coming out here tonight, you're sending a signal to the city. A signal that we're not going to stand for this anymore!"

More applause, and a few scattered boos from the hookers. Rosie Corona's bare arms flailed as she stage-whispered directions for the next chant.

Jericho continued: "As you know, this rally was partly organized by City Councilman Quentin Dudley—"

On cue at the mention of Dudley's name, the hookers howled, "Hypocrite! Hypocrite!"

I wondered what that was all about. The reporters around me looked puzzled, too. Jericho broke stride for only a moment.

"I was asked to tell you that Councilman Dudley—"

"Hypocrite! Hypocrite!"

"—can't be here tonight because of a conflict. It is election season, after all."

Boos and hisses from the hookers. The congregation

looked bewildered at this jeering of their hero, Dudley Do-right.

"But the participation of Councilman Dudley—"

"Hypocrite! Hypocrite!"

I thought I saw the merest hint of a smile tug at the corners of Jericho's mouth. Like he'd finally understood the cue.

"—shows city government is interested in what we have to say. They, too, want to see Central Avenue cleaned up. Councilman Dudley—"

"Hypocrite! Hypocrite!"

Jericho paused longer this time, glanced over to the reporters to make sure they were getting this down.

"—has been a leader among men in this struggle. Remember him when it's time to get out there and vote!"

Jericho peered over toward the whirring TV cameras again, looking satisfied, and moved on.

"The politicians pay attention to us now, at election time. But we'll have to keep after them to make sure they follow up on their promises to make Central Avenue a safe place."

Rosie Corona stood before her hookers with her arms raised like a bandleader's, looking over her shoulder at Jericho, waiting for a gap. Jericho wasn't giving her one.

"I suppose many of you have heard the news that another young girl was murdered down here on Central Avenue. How long, O Lord, how long will we allow this killing to continue?"

"Amens" rippled through the crowd.

The hookers started up again: "Slaves no more, we can SCORE! Slaves no more, we can SCORE!"

A few young men had drifted from the congregation and had massed, muttering, on the sidewalk directly across from the hookers. I thought I recognized a couple as being among the guys who'd hustled the drunk away from the last rally. I leaned over to Felicia's ear.

"Things are about to get ugly."

She looked up from her notebook, followed my eyes to the street. Five Christian brown-shirts picked their way through traffic.

I looked for the cops, saw three of them clustered around a squad car at the end of the block. The cops spotted the toughs moving across the wide street about then. They threw down their cigarettes and hurried over toward the crowd, nightsticks in hand. Two others came running from the other end of the block, trying to cut off the men.

The first of Jericho's followers reached the hookers and waded in among them to grab Rosie Corona by the arm. I thought, Big mistake, fella. Rosie wheeled on the man with a hiss and snatched her arm away. The guy looked surprised, took a step back.

Some of the hookers backed away, but one, a six-foot apparition of black skin and hot pink Spandex, swooped out of the crowd and gave the Christian a push in the chest. The guy was taken off guard and he fell to his ass on the sidewalk. The other men edged forward to help, and the black shook a fist at them, egging them on.

I strained my eyes for a better look, and, my God, it was Willis! Or rather, Wilhemina. Or Wilma or Willow or whatever the hell name he was going by tonight. Recognizing him gave me a brief, crazy urge to run over there and help him protect those hookers. Just because we'd fought on the same side ten years ago. Go figure. Anyway, I was able to control myself, even when the cops moved in and roughly pushed Willis out of the way. The cops formed a ragged line between the men and the hookers, keeping them separated, and one ordered the men back across the street.

"What happened over there?" It was Felicia at my elbow, standing on her tiptoes, trying to see.

I remembered what Willis had said about the contents of his purse. "The cops just kept those Christians from getting sliced to ribbons."

"Really?"

Jericho's voice had been booming the whole time, but most people, like me, had been distracted, wondering who all was going to jail. Looked like no one, though the cops were talking it over among themselves. One of them detached and started making his way to Jericho's stage.

"Some might say it is the Lord striking these sinners down," the reverend shouted. "But, lo, I say unto you, brothers and sisters, it is Satan's work."

I rolled my eyes, thinking, Here we go again.

"As long as this miles-long den of iniquity is allowed to continue—"

Jericho caught the cop out of the corner of his eye. The cop reached the end of the stage, started up the steps.

"—no one is safe."

Jericho broke off, stepped quickly across the stage toward the cop, scowling over the interruption.

The preacher held the microphone behind his back while he had a whispered conference with the cop. Jericho shook his head a couple of times, but the cop prevailed and the preacher stepped away from him, raised the microphone to his lips.

"Because of all the *disturbances,*" he said pointedly, "the police have asked us to call an early halt to our rally."

The crowd groaned in disappointment. Just when things were getting good.

"Let's finish with one last hymn," he said. He swung his arm to crank up the choir. "Mine eyes have seen the glory of the coming of the Lord . . ."

I looked to the hookers to see what Rosie Corona had up her sleeve next. But most of them had scattered after the trouble, and Rosie couldn't get the remaining few organized into anything. Not with that old familiar war hymn booming across at them like artillery. Willis had disappeared.

Beside me, Felicia looked at her watch. "I've got to go. If I hurry, I can still make the first edition."

"Will I see you later?"

"Afraid not," she said. "This will take another hour or two, and I'm already beat."

She edged away, not wanting me to kiss her in front of her colleagues. I gave her an awkward little wave and she was gone through the singing congregation.

Once the hymn was over, the crowd beat it for their cars, trying to get off Central Avenue before it got too dark. I spotted Jericho's blow-dried head ducking into a long black car parked behind the portable stage. He looked angry.

I sauntered through the vanishing crowd to Central. Rosie Corona still was across the street, picking up discarded signs with a couple of her girls. I trotted through the traffic toward her, thinking I'd ask her what all that "hypocrite" stuff was about, but she spotted me before I reached the sidewalk. She straightened up, put her hands on her hips.

"Well, looky here," she said. "It's Baby's favorite food."

The two hookers straightened, looked me over with hard eyes.

"I was wondering if I could talk to you—"

"Forget about it."

The hookers moved closer to Rosie, protecting her flanks. I stood there gulping like a fish, trying to think of something else to say. Rosie Corona was ready with the one thing guaranteed to run me off.

"Girls, meet Sultan Sweeney's newest whore."

19

I awoke early from a nightmare about Lorrie Quintana dancing an awkward hula in the nude, her popped eyes dangling and bouncing on her cheeks. By the time I untangled from the sheets, took a leak, and got a drink of water, I was wide awake.

There's not much a private investigator can do when the rest of the world is still asleep. You don't go knocking on doors before dawn unless you're looking to get shot. I would've gladly gone back to sleep, but there seemed to be no escape from the murder case there.

I fumbled into my bathrobe and made some coffee and padded around my room, thinking. Maybe my problem was a lack of organization. I'd just wandered from one place to another, asking questions, getting in trouble, without a formal game plan. Maybe if I spread out all my notes and clippings on the floor, arranged them in some kind of order, I could make sense of the murders.

I started with my notebook, tearing out pages and slapping them in place on the floor until it began to resemble a huge game of solitaire. Then it was on to the bottom dresser drawer that I call my filing system.

My business files—tax information, licenses, bankbooks—are all in good order, erect and alphabetical in their end of the drawer. The rest is a jumble of fat file folders with cryptic labels like SEX and SURVEILLANCE and MURDER.

I was sitting on the floor, my third cup of coffee at my knee, thumbing through SEX, when I found a long-forgotten article I'd clipped from the *Gazette* a couple of years earlier. I moved to my easy chair to read it under better light.

By nine I was driving west on Central toward the University of New Mexico, early for my hastily arranged appointment with Dr. David Morton.

Morton, according to the clipping, was a psychologist who'd had some success treating sex offenders in an experimental program at UNM. The article said he used therapy and something called behavioral conditioning to turn them around. I couldn't make sense of all of it, but one thing was clear: Here was a guy who understood perverts.

I located the tree-ringed Psychology building, parked the Chevy, and followed the directions Morton had given me to his basement lab. I stepped into a dim hallway, found nothing but closed doors to greet me.

"Dr. Morton?" Quietly. I didn't know what I might be disturbing, whether some sex fiend might jump out through one of the doors.

Instead, the door to my right was opened quickly by a wiry guy with wiry hair and wire-rimmed glasses. He shushed me before I could say anything more, and pulled me into the booth where he was working.

After he shut the door, Morton shook my hand. It was close in the booth, a walk-in closet filled with humming equipment: a tape recorder, a slide projector, a video camera, a strip chart machine with a bouncing needle, like a polygraph.

Dominating the wall was a two-way mirror looking into the next room. In there, a young blond man sat in a Barcalounger under a sheet, facing away from us, watching images flashing on the wall from the slide projector.

"This subject," Morton whispered, "is nearly done, and then we can talk."

An image of a young girl, maybe six years old, flashed onto the screen. She was sitting very still, her hands in her lap and the tip of an adult penis in her mouth. Only the adult's hairy crotch was visible at the side of the slide. It was a horrible image. One of those things, like a mutilated corpse, you know instantly will be with you for life.

"Jesus!"

"Sshhh. If he hears someone else in here, it'll screw up the results."

"Sorry," I whispered. "What exactly are you doing here?"

"That man has a plethysmograph attached to his penis."

"A what?" It sounded like the man had been attacked by a crustacean.

"A plethysmograph. We call it a peter meter."

"Peter meter?"

"Yeah. It's a little metal band, fits around the penis, measures arousal. It's connected to this machine."

He pointed to the strip chart. The needle had swung wildly while the little girl's slide was on the screen.

"Hmm," Morton said. "He's still spiking on that one."

I kept my eyes averted, not wanting to see any more of the twisted images.

"So, what do you do, give his peter a shock?"

Morton smiled, like he'd often had that thought.

"No, nothing like that. It's just a way of telling us if the therapy's working. Plus, we talk into his headphones. Say he gets aroused over that slide of the little girl. I can tell him about flashing police lights and arrest and getting his name in the newspaper as a child molester. That can turn off his fantasy."

The booth went dark, and I realized the show was over. Morton said, "Wait here."

He went outside, closed the door behind him. Through the mirror, I watched the blond guy reach under the sheet and detach the ring from his penis. He zipped up just as Morton entered.

"How'd I do, Doc?"

"Better, but we still have some work to do."

The blond clamped his mouth shut, nodded. He and Morton disappeared from view around the corner, and I waited for the shrink to return.

After a few minutes Morton opened the door and led me down a hall to his office. He sat behind a cluttered desk, put his feet up, gestured me into a chair.

"Now what can I do for you?"

"First of all, I'm sorry if I messed up your session. I guess I was a little early."

"No problem. He didn't see you, and that's the main thing. We don't want to lose his trust."

"So what did that guy do? Is he a child molester?"

Morton nodded, seemed unbothered by the question.

"He's much better. When he came to us, he could barely interact with an adult. He only related to children. So when his sex drive got the better of him, it was children he sought out. We've taught him social skills, how to carry on a conversation. Now we're working on what arouses him, trying to change it."

"And this peter meter helps?"

"Well, it helps us measure what arouses the guy. Say I show a film of a rape on the screen." I made a face. "A lot of men would get turned on by that, actually. You'd be surprised. Anyway, we're not measuring whether that arouses him as much as we're comparing that arousal against what he gets when we show him a normal, loving sex scene."

I was beginning to get it.

"And you use this on rapists, too?"

Morton shook his head. "Only on child molesters, ones with no violence in their history. They're carefully screened. If one guy leaves our program and goes out and rapes or kills somebody, we're dead in the water. We only accept about one-tenth of the men who apply."

"And it gets them on the street faster?"

"Once we're sure they're going to be okay out there."

"Do you work with rapists at all?"

"I have. But not with this method. With child molesters, you're dealing with maladaptive behaviors. With rapists, it's all anger and power. They're too unpredictable to let loose on the streets. In fact, I don't think the prisons keep most of them long enough."

I scratched my chin. I wasn't sure this guy could help me, but he seemed to know more about this stuff than I'd ever want to learn.

I told him I was tracking down the guy who was stalking hookers on the Cruise. He'd read about the murders in the newspapers and it didn't take long to fill in the details.

When I finished, Morton stared at the papers on his desk for a moment, shook his head.

"A very sick individual."

"You said it."

"It's significant the first killing was the transvestite, if we can assume all of them were murdered by the same person."

"Which we don't know for sure."

"Right. But say they were. Guy picks up a prostitute, maybe gets a blow job, decides to go back to her room. When they get there, he finds out she's a he. That could make a guy snap. Especially if he already had sexual problems."

"What kind of problems?"

"You know, the usual. He'd already have questions about his own sexuality. Maybe he's a virgin or a severely repressed homosexual. Or a person who was molested as a child and since has suppressed all sexual fantasies. Someone who's never had a successful sexual relationship."

"Is that all? There's a jillion guys like that walking around."

"Yes, but most don't turn to violence. Once a guy starts mutilating his victims, it's a pretty sure bet he's a goner. That's too much to overcome, even with the best therapy."

That gave me an idea.

"Sometimes, at these murder scenes, people report they've heard bawling, you know, loud weeping. I'd always assumed it was the girls, but it could've been him, huh?"

"Sure, that fits. The guy might feel terribly guilty about what he'd done. After it was over. During the act, he's probably in a sort of blind rage. Out of his head. After he comes back to himself, sees what he's done, it might make him cry."

Deena's corpse flashed through my mind like the pornographic images on the lab screen. I shook my head, thanked Morton, got to my feet. As I was going out the door I remembered one more thing I'd meant to ask him.

"What about a religious fanatic of some kind? Could there be a connection?"

Morton nodded. "Sure. Religion fills an emotional need the same way sex does. When the two collide, bad things happen."

Out in the sunshine, among the sleepy Monday morning coeds and hurrying calculator types, I took a deep breath. I felt shaky as I walked over to my car, like it had been me under that sheet, being measured, judged.

It was hot in the car and I rolled down the windows and sat there, my hand on the ignition key. Something in what Morton had said niggled me, chased around in the back of my mind. I walked through our conversation, ticking off the factors he'd said could make a guy ripe for perverted murder.

One thing became clear: Someone filled with that much hate, no matter how guilty he might feel later, is someone who'd never been loved.

I knew someone who fit that description.

20

I was home before I knew it. I felt I understood the who and the why now, but the hows and whens seemed to swim in the air around me, just out of reach. And those were what I needed for proof.

I hurried into my room and picked up notebook pages off the floor until I found the notes I'd taken during my conversation with Lieutenant Steve Romero. I checked the times of the murders. Some were estimates, but they were well within the range I thought I'd need. In the morning; most of the murders had occurred in the morning. Only Felix the transvestite and young Deena had been killed at night. I pushed stuff off the top of my dresser until I located a calendar. Monday nights. They'd both been killed on Monday nights.

Then I called Sultan Sweeney.

"Hullo?" He came on the line sleepy, with none of his usual cold formality.

"Sweeney? It's Bubba Mabry."

"Bubba? What de hell do you want? What time is it?"

"Is Hughie there?"

"What? Hughie? Naw, he never comes to work till noon. What do you want with him?"

My pulse quickened. "Does he get a night off?"

"What? What's dis all about, Mabry?"

"Goddammit, what's his night off?"

"Mondays. Today's Monday, isn't it? Today is his day off, awright? What you so excited about?"

"Hughie did it, Sweeney. Hughie killed those girls."

"Get outta here."

"I'm sure of it. Listen. All the killings were in the morning, except for two, and both of those were on Monday nights."

I heard bedsprings squeak, like Sultan Sweeney was struggling to sit up.

"Hell, dat don't prove nothin'."

"I talked to a shrink this morning, a guy who specializes in sex criminals. You know what he said? The killer was likely some guy who'd never had a love life."

"Yeah, so?"

"You told me yourself Hughie never even had a friend until you came along."

"But what does dat have to do—"

"Shut up and listen. You come along and become his friend, give him a job. Suddenly, all these good-looking hookers are parading through his life. And he can't even touch them, never has been able to touch a woman. You follow me?"

"I'm with you." Serious now, sober.

"Finally, one night, a woman shows an interest in him, tells him he has a nice smile, doesn't mind that his skin looks like a freaking mine field. Hughie can't believe it. He's so excited he's about to burst. And he gets back to the woman's apartment, and they're taking off their clothes in the dark, and the woman turns out to be a man."

"What?"

"A man, Sweeney. Drag queen name of Felix."

"Oh, shit." He'd heard about Felix.

"That's right. Hughie snaps. Suddenly, he's not your silent friend anymore. He's your competitor. He probably tried to hit on the girls when you weren't looking. He's motivated now, feels like he's got to prove he's a man."

"Ah, Jesus—"

"Say he shows up at a girl's door. She'd think you sent him, some kind of business. She lets him in, and he tries to make a move on her. Clumsy, probably. Remember, he's never done this before. The woman would freak when he tried to touch her. She'd scream, maybe, and he couldn't have that. Couldn't have you finding out what he'd been up to. You're his only friend."

Silence filled the telephone line, like Sultan was holding his breath on the other end. Finally, there was a rush of expelled air, almost a moan.

"What do we do now?" he said.

"Where's Hughie?"

"I don't know. Home, I guess. He's got an apartment near here."

"We've got to find him."

"Sure, but I'm still in bed."

"Listen, Sweeney, the murders have been getting closer together. Do you understand? First, he was waiting weeks between killings. Now it's days. There's no time to waste."

"Awright, awright. Hold on. I'll call him on de other line."

There was a click and a hum, and I was on hold. I cracked my knuckles against the phone receiver at my ear. They sounded loud and hollow. Another click, and Sultan was back on the line.

"Nobody home."

"Okay, get some clothes on, and I'll pick you up. We need to track him down."

I hung up. I got the Smith & Wesson out of the nightstand drawer and clipped the holster to my belt. I looked around my room to see what I was forgetting, had my hand on the doorknob before something else occurred to me. I dialed the phone again.

Felicia answered with a brusque, automatic "Quattlebaum," like she was at the office rather than at home, probably still in bed, sleeping late like Sultan Sweeney.

"How would you like a big story?"

"Bubba?"

"Yeah, it's me. You want to be on the front page tomorrow?"

"With what?"

"I know who killed the hookers."

"Oh boy. Are you sure?"

"I'll be right over. Pick you up on the street."

My pulse pounded in my ears while I raced through traffic to Felicia's place. She waited at the curb, looking thrown together in T-shirt and jeans. She had a camera bag slung over her shoulder. I drove past her, did a U-turn, stopped with the passenger door dead in front of her.

She flung open the door and threw in her camera bag.

"The back," I snapped. "Get in the back."

"Why?"

"We've got to pick up Sultan Sweeney next."

"Why don't we do this ourselves?"

"He's the client. Get in the back."

She scowled, but huffed her way into the cluttered backseat.

"If you use that thing," I said, pointing at the camera bag, "make sure you don't get Sweeney in the picture."

"How come?"

"Afraid he'll insist on that. In fact, it might be better if you didn't take any photos until the police arrive."

"You're calling the police?"

"If we can find the guy. You should see him. He's big as a house. Let the cops handle him."

I sped away, explaining about Hughie over my shoulder, getting a good case of chauffeur's neck. I adjusted the mirror so I could see her while I talked. Her head was down in concentration as she rocked to the potholes. She was writing down everything I said. That made me stumble. Was this a good idea, bringing her along? I finished my point about the timing of the murders, and she looked up and met my eyes in the mirror. She grinned at me, her face flushed. Yeah, it was a good idea.

Only thirty minutes passed between the time I hung up the phone with Sultan Sweeney and the time we arrived at his house in Ridgecrest. Still, he was pacing on the porch when we got there, decked out in a loose-fitting, five-hundred-dollar suit and sipping from a china coffee cup.

Sultan set the cup on a table and sprang down the steps, graceful as a panther. He stopped short when he reached my side of the car and saw Felicia in the backseat.

"Who's dat?"

"Sultan Sweeney, meet Felicia Quattlebaum."

"Who?"

"She's a reporter with the *Gazette.*"

"A re*por*ter? What de hell you doin' to me, Bubba?"

"We owe her. I couldn't have solved this thing without her. Get in."

"I'm not ridin' with any reporter."

"She's, uh, also my girlfriend." God, it sounded silly.

Sultan leaned with his hands on my door. He glared at Felicia another few seconds, then shrugged his shoulders.

"Don't know why I'm objectin'," he said, the chill back in his voice. "We ain't gonna find Hughie anyhow. If he's not home, I don't know where to look for him."

"We'll find him. Get in." I was beginning to sound like John Wayne. My head pounded from the excitement and the arguing and all the rushing around. Sultan put that icy glare on me, but after a second he could see it wasn't having any effect and he turned it off and jogged around the car to the passenger door.

He gave me directions to Hughie's apartment, all the time looking around at the interior of the Chevy, with its tattered upholstery and its sunburned dash.

"Don't let anyone see me in dis car."

"What's the matter with this car?" Felicia demanded from the backseat.

He turned in his seat to look at her. "You got a mouth on you, too. Looks like you found a perfect match, Bubba."

Felicia made a sound like a growl in her throat.

"You two just cool it," I said. "I'm trying to pay attention to the road. I don't need to hear a lot of are-we-there-yet."

I wheeled the Chevy onto Hughie's street. He lived on the second floor of a typical Albuquerque low-rent apartment house, a concrete cube with iron balconies across the front. I parked and turned to Sultan Sweeney.

"Why don't you go knock on his door. Just see if he's home. Tell him you need him to work today, something like that."

"He's off on Mondays."

"Tell him to meet you later. Make something up.

Then just hurry back down here and we'll call the cops."

"I don't want any cops. I want to talk to Hughie."

"Just go knock on the freaking door. If he's still not home, none of this matters."

Sultan shrugged, slipped out of the car. Felicia slid across the backseat behind me, and I could feel her breath on my neck as we watched Sultan glide up the stairs. He knocked on an apartment door, waited, knocked again. Nothing.

"How do we know that's Hughie's apartment?" Felicia said to the back of my head. "How do we know he isn't scamming us?"

"You heard him. He wants to talk to Hughie, sort this thing out."

Sultan came back down the stairs.

"Look at him," she said. "He's too slick. He looks like a killer to me."

"Jesus. Don't start up with him, okay?"

"Okay, okay." She fell back in the seat with a huff.

Sultan climbed into the car. "What do we do now?"

"Where else might he be? Where does he eat breakfast? Where's he wash his clothes?"

"I told you. I don't know any of dat. He just works for me."

That slowed me up. "Think. He must've said something in the past. Anything."

"You know Hughie. He don't say much."

Felicia sighed loudly, like she'd known all along we'd end up stumped.

"Okay, look, he's probably around Central someplace," I said. "We'll go warn your girls to stay away from him, keep their doors locked, and we'll keep an eye out for his car."

Much grumbling all around, but nobody came up with a better idea, so we roared away toward the cheap motels of the Cruise.

21

Our first stop was the Shifting Sands Motor Inn, a flat-roofed monstrosity that looked cockeyed, all its windows slightly off square, like it should've been called the Shifting Foundation Motor Inn.

Sultan Sweeney pointed me into a parking slot, said, "Wait here," and got out of the car. He pounded on a nearby door until it was opened by a woman I didn't know, a bosomy redhead in a bathrobe, her hair mussed and her eyelids heavy with sleep. She snapped to attention when she saw it was Sweeney, made gestures like she was inviting him in, then listened as he talked quickly. Only some of the words drifted as far as the car where I waited with Felicia.

"Oh yeah," she said, nudging the back of my seat with her foot, "this will be on the front page tomorrow. No question."

Without turning around, I said, "We can take you home if you like."

"Oh, no, I wouldn't miss this for the world. Riding around with a pimp, checking on his employees, before breakfast."

"Would you rather we didn't warn these girls? Today's Monday, Hughie's day off. He's got a whole day to get up a head of steam and go after another one."

That shut her up. She scribbled a few notes, sighed some more. Sweeney returned to the car, a little excitement leaking through his cool exterior.

"She hasn't seen him."

"You told her to keep her door locked?"

"Yeah, yeah, let's go."

"Where to?"

"Over to de Paradise. Where de other girls are staying."

"All of them?"

Sultan let the silence lie heavy in the car. "Ain't dat many left."

It wasn't far to the Paradise Motel. Sultan explained on the way over that he'd persuaded all his girls—all but the redhead, who was a longtime resident of the Shifting Sands—to move to the Paradise after the killings started. So they could keep an eye on each other.

"Didn't work so well for Lorrie Quintana, did it?"

I couldn't help myself. If I'd known he'd put them all in one place, it would've saved me a lot of running around earlier. He should've told me.

Sultan jumped out of the car once we reached the Paradise and started his door-pounding routine. The hooker who calls herself Melody opened the first door, already dressed for work in hot pants and camisole. She glanced over at our car, but I resisted an urge to wave. I could feel Felicia's eyes on the back of my head. The less I had to explain later, the better.

Melody shook her head a couple of times, nodded, then closed her door. Sultan hurried down the sidewalk away from us, passing several doors before reaching the next one where one of his women waited. He raised his hand to knock, but the hand froze in midair. He cocked his head, listening, then dug into his pockets and came up with his keys.

"Uh-oh," Felicia said behind me.

"Looks like something's up," I agreed, and popped open the car door.

Always the southern gentleman, I held the seat forward while Felicia dragged the camera bag out of the back, but my eyes were on Sweeney. He fiddled with his keys, gently unlocked the door. Then he snaked a pistol out from under his coat and pushed the door open.

"Hey!" I shouted. "Sweeney! Wait!"

I ran around the car and down the sidewalk, fishing out my gun as I ran. Felicia's feet slapped behind me.

Before I reached the door I could hear what Sultan had heard. Howling. Hoarse bawling like a cow caught in a fence. A horrible sound that pulled me up short. Felicia crashed into me, nearly bowled me over. We got untangled and I waved at her to show her to stay back. Then I took a deep breath and ducked through the door, gun held high in both hands, just like the cops in the movies.

Two steps into the dim room, then into a squat, gun barrel moving with my eyes. What I saw made my mouth fall open, my gun barrel droop.

Hughie sat cross-legged in the bed, naked except for a pair of wide briefs, his hairless, pasty, oozing skin exposed to the air and reeking. His mouth was open and his bright red face contorted with his sobs. He was a grotesque baby, bawling in his crib, stroking the hand of a dead whore.

My eyes ran up her body, past bottle-tanned legs and bare hips and a ripped camisole. Her hair was over her face, but I recognized her as Side Street Sally, the hooker with designs on Sultan Sweeney, the one for whom prostitution was a temporary means to a happy ending. Her cheek was the color of a plum, and her neck bent at a funny angle, and she was as dead as her plans for a Las Vegas wedding. If her friends could see her now.

Sweeney stood off to my right, his feet wide, his gun pointed at Hughie's face. His mouth twisted down in anger and his eyes were cold. The gun trembled ever so slightly in his hands.

Felicia's shadow fell from the doorway to the green carpet at my feet. She gave a little gasp as her eyes adjusted from the bright sunlight. Having her there reminded me I needed to do something more than gawk.

"Take it easy, Sultan." It wasn't much, but it was all that occurred to me. It distracted him ever so slightly.

"Shut up, Mabry."

Hughie shrieked even louder. I didn't know a grown man could cry like that.

"Hughie!" Sultan barked it, and Hughie clamped his mouth shut, swallowed the howl like it was dry oatmeal. His breath came finally in great shudders, but he wasn't bawling anymore.

Felicia said from the door: "What's the matter with his skin?"

Hughie hiccuped, looked like he was ready to let go again. Sultan wheeled on Felicia, pointed the pistol at her face.

"Would you all please shut *up?*"

Felicia gulped.

My own gun was pointed at the floor, frozen there as securely as an anchor chain in the Antarctic.

Sultan's eyes swung from Felicia to me to the bed, where Hughie still held the hand of the late Sally. The pistol never wavered from its aim on Felicia.

"While we're at it, Mabry," he said, "why don't you

drop your gun? I don't want no one makin' a mistake."

I had no choice. I bent at the knees, let the gun fall a couple of feet to the carpet.

"Now, you," he said to Felicia, "get in here and shut dat door."

The door gobbled up the shaft of sunlight, and it was much darker in there, and Hughie let a quaking sob escape. Sultan, in control now, turned back to him, pointed the pistol.

"You don't have to shoot him, Sultan," I said. "He's not going anywhere."

"Wrong, Mabry. He's goin' straight to Hell."

I saw the muscles in his shoulder tighten through his suit, like I could watch the nerve function run down his arm from his brain to his trigger finger. Then I was off my feet, flying at him, no freaking idea what I'm doing. I crashed into his arm as the gun went off and Hughie screamed behind me and Sultan and I fell to the carpet in a tangle of elbows and knees.

The pistol was loose on the floor. Sultan got a hand on my face and bent back my neck. I struck at him blindly, not punching, more like thrashing at him with my forearms. A knee caught me in the short ribs, sent a wave of pain through me like all my internal organs had been jarred out of place. I gasped and clutched at him and tried to roll him over, to get my weight on top, awkward as a gator wrestler.

Felicia danced around us. She'd dropped her camera bag somewhere, but it apparently hadn't occurred to her to pick up my gun and get this insanity under control. She was looking for a place to jump on the pile.

I turned my head to instruct her, and Sultan socked me one under the jaw that made me see lights. Then he rolled me back the other way, tried to break free from my grip, still scrambling for his pistol. From nowhere something cracked against the side of my head and the lights flashed again and everything went dark.

I came to in Felicia's arms, my head cradled in her lap.

"Bubba, I'm so sorry."

I didn't know what she meant. I blinked my eyes and tried to focus, tried to find Sultan Sweeney. Hughie howled and hiccuped behind us like an ambulance.

"What happened?"

"I kicked you in the head. It was an accident. I'm really, really sorry."

Sultan Sweeney stepped into view, kept clear of my legs. He pointed the pistol toward Hughie and shouted, "Shut de fuck up!"

Hughie choked and sputtered and sobbed, but he managed to crank down the volume.

With most men, it would've been enough. That kind of interruption, only a minute or two, would give them time for second thoughts, make them slow to pull the trigger. But Sultan Sweeney standing over me, all rumpled suit and viper eyes, looked ready to plug all three of us.

"Come on, Sultan," I said from the floor, "you don't want this. It isn't your style."

"What de fuck you know 'bout my style?" His anxiety showed in his voice, the Cajun poling its pirogue ever thicker into his accent. It was getting very close to nut-cutting time.

Think! I told myself. And the word seemed to echo in my head.

Sultan looked back toward Hughie. "How come you do dis to me, boy?"

I heard a gasp behind me as Hughie tried to answer, then the dam broke again and great shuddering sobs filled the room.

Sultan rolled his eyes. "God*damn!* Will you shut dat noise up?"

"Listen to him, Sultan," I said. "You can hear him for a city block. There was that shot. The cops'll be here any second."

"Dey gonna find a mess."

"Don't make it any worse than it is. You can just walk away."

Sultan allowed himself a snort. "Too late for dat."

"No it isn't. You said yourself you could just walk away and leave all this. Walk out that door, around the corner, catch a cab. The cops come, you were never here."

"You think dat reporter gonna keep it to herself?"

"She won't say a word, won't write it in the newspaper."

Felicia tensed under me. "Now, wait a minute—"

"Not a word."

Felicia took a deep breath, and I felt her relax, accept it. She said, "Not a word."

Then she pinched my ear, hard enough to make me say "Ow!"

Sultan looked at us like we were stupid, playing around so close to death. He sighed, blinked.

"Where would I go? The cops'll never leave me alone now."

"They'll hunt you a lot harder if you shoot somebody. You can find someplace to vanish. You did it before."

I rose up on an elbow. Slowly.

"I'll keep a gun on Hughie until the cops arrive."

Sultan squinted at the ceiling, sighed, still not sure. Felicia and I held our breaths. Hughie moaned and whimpered.

"Ah, hell, why not? Mosta my harem's gone anyway. Includin' dis sweet little girl here. I can't believe it."

He let his gun arm fall. He stepped lightly to the door and was gone, quick and smooth.

Felicia exhaled loudly. I rolled over, got to my knees, and crawled over to my pistol before Hughie could catch his breath enough to try and escape.

Felicia and I sat on the floor, gasping with adrenaline and fear.

"You know," she said, "it would've been a better story if you'd let him go ahead and shoot this brute. Fewer trials to cover later."

"I couldn't have done that. And he wouldn't have let us go after we'd seen it."

"But to let him just walk away! He's responsible for all this, for putting these women in jeopardy."

I shook my head to show her I wasn't going to bite. She sighed, rolled her eyes toward the ceiling.

Then the door burst open and sunlight spilled in, and two shadowy cops pointed guns at us. Hughie screamed in surprise.

"Police. Drop the gun."

I did it.

"Now," the cop said, stepping sideways into the room, "you're all under arrest."

22

It took a while to sort it all out.

The cops handcuffed us and read us our rights. I talked all over the part about remaining silent, but they ignored my explanations.

No way they could fit a handcuff around Hughie's pulpy wrist, so they ordered him out of the bed and against the wall and kept their guns trained on him. Other cops arrived. They locked Felicia and me in separate squad cars, which was fine by me. Better than listening to her holler about her First Amendment rights.

I sat on my cuffed hands until Romero arrived. He had the uniforms hoist me out of the car, and leaned me against a fender while he got the whole story. Everything except any mention of Sultan Sweeney. Which was, naturally, the one thing he asked when I was done.

"Did Sweeney know who was killing these girls?"

I shook my head, swallowed.

"He still doesn't know. I haven't even seen him. As soon as I figured out it was Hughie, I tracked him here. All of Sweeney's girls are staying here."

He stared at me with doubting eyes, waited for me to crack. My jaw was clamped so tight my teeth got shorter.

"And you brought along your girlfriend?"

"I told her it might be a big story. I'm trying to get in good with her."

"Well, getting her arrested is quite a start."

"Arrested? But I told you, we caught the guy."

"Until they hear it all Downtown, you're both still in custody."

"Can you at least take off the cuffs? They pinch."

"Tough."

We rode to the police station in a caravan of squad cars.

Hughie sniffled, but was otherwise quiet as the uniforms herded him into the booking area, none of them quite touching him. The cops had let him slip on a shirt over his underwear, but his fat bare legs and red face oozed and stank.

Romero marched Felicia and me through the halls to Homicide. Felicia quacked over her shoulder about how stupid Romero would look in tomorrow's *Gazette,* but it had no effect on him. Romero's like those fish that lie on the bottom of the ocean, looking for all the world like craggy stones. Until some critter wanders too close, then the stone splits open and, whomp, he's lunch. Romero's face cracked only to tell us "Turn left" or "In here."

Our destination was the office of Romero's new boss, LeRoy Schulte, which was sealed off from the rest of the Homicide squad room by walls of frosted glass. Romero swung the door open and pointed us in. As I passed his chin, he muttered something, sounded like, "Good luck." My heart sank.

Schulte stood ramrod straight, his fingertips resting on his desktop. He wore a striped tie and a white shirt with long sleeves. And gold cuff links. The cuff links told me everything I needed to know about Schulte: He was the kind of cop who'd given up on being a cop to focus on becoming chief. He probably practiced Rotary Club speeches in front of the mirror while he shaved three times a day. No wonder Romero hated him.

Romero stood at parade rest just inside the closed door while Schulte waved us into chairs. Schulte had our names written on a sheet of paper on his desk blotter, and he read them off and looked at each of us, seeing if we objected to his pronunciations. He sat down stiffly and began.

"Now, I'd like to hear about how the two of you ended up in a motel room with a murder victim."

I opened my mouth, but Felicia cut me off.

"I believe I'm entitled to a phone call."

Schulte stuck out his chin at her, but said nothing until his voice was under perfect control.

"Lieutenant, would you accompany Miss Quattlebaum to the pay phone? I'll see what Mr. Mabry has to say while you're gone."

He arched his eyebrows at me, like he was asking whether that would be all right with me, all on the up and up. That's when I noticed the tape recorder at his elbow, its little reels slowly turning. He was keeping a careful record of everything he did, everything that was said, so he wouldn't be to blame if anything went wrong with the case. Being that careful must have put a lot of pressure on him, and that worried me a little. I'd almost rather had Captain Morgan shouting into my face, like in the old days. At least I knew how to play him.

"Where do you want me to start?"

Schulte steepled his fingers, studied his manicure. "How about at the beginning?"

"Okay, but it'll take longer that way. As far as I'm concerned, this all began a couple of weeks ago when I found the body of a girl named Deena at my motel."

I meant to throw him off the scent of Sultan Sweeney, to get him thinking about my own involvement instead of who my client might be. But as I talked, I realized it was true. After I'd found Deena's body, I'd been depressed, sleepless, fighting with Felicia. Once I'd started searching for Deena's murderer, I had more energy. I mean, there still were distasteful moments, times when I was confused or hurting or mopey, but overall I'd felt more alive once I'd begun the hunt. There was a serious question about me somewhere in there, but I filed it away for later, concentrated on telling my story to Schulte.

I explained about the times of the murders, how most of the victims had worked for the same guy Hughie worked for (without mentioning Sultan by name), how I'd known where to look for the moldering giant once I'd decided he was the killer.

"What happened," he asked when I paused, "when you arrived at the motel room?"

"Oh." I gathered my thoughts. "I heard him bawling through the door, so I kicked it open and jumped inside and got the drop on him. He was unarmed, sitting up in bed with the dead woman. I told Miss Quattlebaum to call the police, but a couple of uniforms burst in before she got to the phone. Then we came here."

"The arresting officers say the door didn't look forced."

I shrugged. "Maybe it was unlocked. I didn't have to kick it very hard."

"Why did you go in at all? Why didn't you just call us?"

"I heard someone in distress. I didn't know if there was time."

"There's a bullet hole in the wall of that room."

"Really? I wouldn't know anything about that. My gun hasn't been fired."

He paused, tried to stare me down.

"You didn't stage all this for that reporter?"

My porch light finally came on. He was less worried about what had happened than about what would appear in the *Gazette*. This was his front-page murder case, the one that had the mayor chewing on his neck. And somebody else had caught the killer.

"I wouldn't have brought her along if I'd known what we were going to find. I was just knocking on doors, and happened onto it. She was there. There was no stopping her. Wait till you talk to her. You'll see what I mean."

The office door opened and Felicia harrumphed in, Romero's hand on her elbow. She was no longer handcuffed, but she was madder than ever.

"I wasn't finished with my phone call!"

"You were finished." Romero thrust her into her chair, a little roughly, I thought, and then he turned to Schulte. "She was dictating a story to somebody at the paper. I figured that wouldn't be what you wanted."

Schulte's hands did a little dance around his desktop, searching for something to strangle. "This is a police matter, Miss Quattle—"

"I wasn't finished. I'm entitled to one phone call, and I was still making it."

"That privilege is for calling your lawyer, not your editor."

"I can call anyone I like." Felicia's voice dropped to a withering burn. I knew that tone. Anything could happen now. What a bad time to be in handcuffs.

Then she surprised me. She took a deep breath, crossed her legs, plucked at something on her sleeve.

"Besides," she said, "they're sending our lawyer. I'll

be out of here in time to write it myself for the first edition."

Schulte's cheeks reddened. His hands set upon each other, clutching and twisting, while he tried to regain his calm.

"This is not a game, Miss Quattlebaum," he said through clenched teeth. "This is a homicide investigation. If you write anything that could screw up the investigation, let the murderer go free, do you think you could live with yourself?"

Her foot bobbed and she glanced around the room like she was hunting a pestering housefly.

"Let me worry about my conscience, Captain," she said. "The guy was caught in the act. Nothing could screw up this investigation. Not even you."

I braced my feet against the floor in case he sprang across the desk. But Schulte just did more silent imploding, the flush spreading on his neck, his eyes blinking rapidly. I thought he'd pop a vein in his head.

Someone knocked on the door, and Romero swung it open to admit Buster Wilson, a blustery, red-nosed Saint Bernard of a man who's been the *Gazette's* lawyer for years. Buster swooped into the room, papers hanging out of his fat briefcase, looking at his watch and panting.

"Amazing! I made it in five minutes. I was just next door at City Hall when my beeper went off—"

"Mr. Wilson," Schulte interrupted, coming to his feet. "I assume you're here to represent Miss Quattlebaum. If you'd just wait outside—"

"Miss Quattlebaum? I'm here to represent both these fine citizens."

I wasn't sure whether to be relieved. Buster the Barrister might be able to bluff his way past a libel jury, but I imagined it had been many years since he'd waltzed into a murder case. One thing we didn't need was somebody else to piss off Schulte.

"You mean," Schulte's voice rose, "Mabry works for the *Gazette?*"

Buster looked puzzled, blinked at me, shook his jowls.

"Why, Captain, to be honest, I don't know anything about Mr. Mabry's employment status. But I know the *Gazette* is outraged at the way he's being treated, sitting there in handcuffs, when everyone knows he's a hero."

Schulte nearly rose up off the floor.

"Miss Quattlebaum, however, is needed on urgent business at the *Gazette.* Unless you're ready to press charges, I'd suggest you remove Mr. Mabry's handcuffs and we'll be on our way."

From up on his toes Schulte said shrilly, "We haven't even taken their statements yet!"

"My clients can't be held responsible for your negligence."

Schulte squeezed his temples, wiped the sweat off his forehead. He looked like he was ready to chew off his own tongue.

"This is police business, Mr. Wilson," he said wearily. "It has to come first. We'll take their statements, then you can have them."

Buster objected some more, but his heart wasn't in it. He'd gotten, I guessed, the best he'd hoped for.

It took a couple of hours for the cops to round up two stenographers and lead Felicia and me into separate rooms and grill us. Since Schulte had already heard what I had to say, had captured it on his cheap tape recorder, I drew Romero as my inquisitor. Buster Wilson stayed with Felicia while Schulte interviewed her. I had no idea what she was saying to him, but I hoped she didn't mention Sultan Sweeney. At least not until Sultan had time to clear out of town. I didn't need him deciding we were unfinished business.

Once we were done, Buster blustered some more,

and Schulte let us go, making it clear he just wanted to be rid of us. As we headed for the door, Romero handed Felicia her camera bag and slipped me my gun.

"No reason for us to hold on to this," he said. I thanked him, and gave Schulte what I hoped was an arch look.

We rode to the *Gazette* building in Buster's car. All the way there he mumbled merrily about his effect on the cops. Felicia scribbled in her notebook, aligning her facts. I rode in the backseat, thinking about Deena and Lorrie and Side Street Sally.

The *Gazette* building is one of those modern jobs that looks like it was assembled from Tinkertoys and Legos. We hurried through the lobby into the big, open newsroom, drawing stares from the fluorescent-lit drones at their desks. Buster marched straight for a door labeled EDITOR, but I trailed Felicia to the city desk.

It was the first time I'd ever been inside the newspaper office. Considering my family history, I'd always thought it prudent to avoid reporters. At least until Felicia came along. I tried to relax, told myself there was nothing I could do. I couldn't very well walk out on Felicia's story, not when things were just beginning to level off between us. Besides, my car was across town at the Paradise Motel. I wondered whether I'd find it up on blocks by the time I got back there.

A little guy with a black goatee rose to his feet as Felicia approached. I read the nameplate on his desk, RICHARD WHITWORTH, CITY EDITOR, and I thought, This is Whitworth? The ogre Felicia always complains about? He wasn't much bigger than Felicia, a stoop-shouldered runt with ink-blackened fingers and bad teeth. The sight of Felicia seemed to make him tired.

Felicia, as usual, got right to the point. "How much space are you holding for this?"

Whitworth swallowed and squinted up at the lights. "As much as McMurray needs."

"McMurray?"

"He's writing the story, Felicia."

"This is *my* story!"

"Yes, but I talked to the brass and we all agreed you're too personally involved. We can't let you take the byline."

"It's mine!"

"It's an ethical problem. This is the way we resolved it."

"Without talking to me first?"

"You were, ah, unavailable."

That set her off. She leaned across the desk and shouted into her boss's face, spitting and snarling and flinging words my mother would find unladylike. She threatened to take her story to another newspaper. She threatened Whitworth's person and the lives of his superiors.

It was awkward, silently waiting there. Like standing by, holding the leash, while your dog chews off somebody's leg.

Whitworth slumped into his chair, watched her impassively until she ran out of breath. Then he leaned forward, put his elbows on his desk.

"Look, Felicia, the fact is, this is a story about you and your boyfriend as much as it is about the murders. You've got a conflict of interest, pure and simple. Now take McMurray into one of the interview rooms, and don't come out until you're done."

She fumed and seethed, but Whitworth stared up at her without blinking. Finally she stalked away toward empty glass-fronted booths that lined one wall of the newsroom. I followed. What else could I do?

A nervous, middle-aged guy with close-set eyes trailed us into one of the rooms and took a chair. I sat down, too, and we introduced ourselves while Felicia paced and smoked.

McMurray, not wanting to tangle with Felicia immediately, got me to tell the story. She sat down finally and began interrupting every so often, interjecting a detail or setting a fact straight. Neither of us mentioned Sultan Sweeney.

After the interview, we were herded into the photo lab, where a bearded photographer stood us up against a blank wall and fired a flash off into our faces. At least, I thought, I'm not holding a row of numbers under my chin.

We trooped back into the newsroom. Felicia looked like she was ready for a final tangle with her editor, but he'd already arranged for a flunky to drive us home, to get us out of his hair while he finished preparing the next day's edition.

The flunky, a college-aged kid who wisely kept his mouth shut, drove us to Felicia's apartment without being told. I didn't object that my car and my home were far away. It seemed better to stay quiet until Felicia got over herself.

She still carried her camera bag as she unlocked her apartment door. She'd lugged the thing around all day without ever firing off a frame. She dumped it on the sofa in the living room, kicked off her shoes, lit another cigarette, paced. Her face was twisted in the same expression of disgust she'd worn since her argument with Whitworth. I couldn't wait until she saw her picture in the paper.

What's a sensitive guy to say at a time like this, when his beloved is frustrated and discouraged? Beats me. I never claimed to be sensitive. In fact, I can usually be counted upon to say the exact wrong thing.

"Well, there's no sense moping. It's over now."

She shot me a go-to-hell look, turned on her heel

and walked over to the sliding glass doors that looked out at her balcony and the mountains beyond.

"You just don't get it, do you?" she said in a voice that could cut glass. "It's not over. Although it'll all be over tomorrow, I suppose."

"Tomorrow?"

"Tomorrow's election day." She didn't add "stupid," but it was implied in her tone.

"What's the election got to do with this? We caught Hughie. You're going to get all the credit in the paper tomorrow. You come off smelling like a rose."

"I come off stinking of a conflict of interest. Even the slow readers will understand why I didn't write that story myself. But that's not the problem."

"It's not?"

"I told you, it's the election. Everything I've been trying to do has been shot down by that gross blob of a murderer."

"How?"

"People read the paper on election day so they'll know which levers to pull. Newspapers always print extra copies for street sales. Everyone will see the story about Hughie."

"Yeah, so?"

"So, it looks like Dudley and Jericho and the rest of those yahoos were right. Scum killing scum, right there on Central Avenue. Dudley will get re-elected by a landslide."

"Maybe so, but that's hardly your fault."

"No, I know. I just didn't want things to turn out this way. I really believed Dudley had something to do with those murders."

She stubbed out her cigarette in an ashtray, giving it an extra mash like it was Whitworth's head.

"Even if they'd let you write the story, you wouldn't have been able to keep Dudley from winning the primary."

"Maybe not. But I could've played down the whole Dudley-turned-out-to-be-right angle. It's all a matter of spin, Bubba. Whitworth's probably on the phone with Dudley right now, letting him put himself in the headlines."

She slumped onto the sofa and stretched out her legs and wiggled her bare toes. She crossed her arms behind her head and sighed. I decided to try something else.

"Don't take this the wrong way, but why does it matter so much? I mean, if reporters are supposed to be impartial, then you shouldn't care who wins the election. Just report the facts and let the voters decide."

She glowered at me, sucked on a tooth, like a horse trader sizing up a jackass.

"I think I've had enough lectures on ethics for one day, thank you."

I nodded, backed up a step. "Right. Sorry."

She let it hang there a second before she said, "Look, Dudley's dirty. I can feel it. Call it a gut feeling, call it animal instinct, call it women's intuition. But I know there's something wrong there. And I'm not going to be able to prove it before they put him into office for another four years."

I plopped down on the sofa next to her, suddenly weary. Standing in for Felicia's editor was a tough job.

And then she surprised me again. She said, "I'm hungry."

Recognizing a distraction, I said quickly, "Me, too. We never had lunch."

"Or breakfast. Let's get some Chinese delivered."

She called a nearby place called Lung Fung and ordered enough food for several large Chinese families. I thought about how this was another advantage to living in the Heights. In my neighborhood, so many people have been mugged, even the pizza joints no longer deliver.

Two hours later Felicia and I sat across from each other, burping and picking our teeth. Little white boxes spilled sauce and stray noodles onto the dining table, and two wine bottles stood empty. We stared out the balcony doors, watching gray creep over the rosy mountains as the sun set.

Through our dinnertime chat, Felicia had come no closer to pinning something on Quentin Dudley, but she seemed to care less. Probably the wine.

I was feeling light-headed, too, the wine overwhelming a throb from the knot Felicia's kick had given me. I bravely got amorous, persuaded her a roll in the sheets was what she needed to take her mind off her disappointments. Of course, that put the pressure on me, didn't it? But I was just drunk enough to feel up to the job. Despite the clumsiness of drink, it all went fine.

We were lying in bed afterward, the sheet pulled up to our chests, Felicia cooing and sighing, me struggling against the wine and that hormone that makes men want to sleep immediately after sex.

"You know, Bubba, I think I've finally figured you out."

That woke me up. "How's that?"

"I was just thinking about how you burst into that motel room today, not knowing what we'd find, whether there'd be shooting."

"Yeah?"

"And I began to understand why you insist on living on Central Avenue."

I struggled to sit up straight. "I don't see—"

"You're a crusader, Bubba. You've staked out that dirty strip as your mission. That's why you have to stay there."

I shook my head. "Not me. I mean, I know a lot of people down there and I'm willing to help the ones who deserve it. But I'm no crusader. I'm not that fervent about anything."

"Admit it. You couldn't leave these murders alone after you found that girl's body, could you?"

She meant Deena. I'd seen so many bodies lately . . .

"I think you're exaggerating."

"Well, it doesn't matter." But she looked smug. "Now that I understand you better, I'll leave you alone about living down there. You stay on Central as long as it takes."

I tried to object some more, but Felicia rolled over, pulled up the covers, and fell fast asleep, a smile on her face.

I lay awake a long time.

23

Sometimes, being a private eye is simply a matter of distributing enough business cards.

Felicia dropped me off at the Paradise Motel a little after ten the next morning. Our night together had improved her mood, and I'd managed to keep her from seeing her *Gazette*. I'd gone outside to fetch it while she was making coffee and had tossed it into some bushes. She'd grumbled about complaining to the circulation office, but that was better than hearing about how McMurray screwed up the story, or how ragged we looked in the mug shots. I figured I could read it later, at a safe distance from Felicia. Like across town.

My Chevy sat in the motel parking lot intact, and I was almost insulted no one had found it desirable enough to strip. I drove home and found a message on my answering machine.

"Mr. Mabry, this is Delbert Winterbottom. Over at Delbert's Dolls? I think I have your missing doll collection here. Give me a call right away."

I dialed the number he'd recited on the message, and his Skilsaw whine answered.

"Oh, Mr. Mabry, I'm so glad to hear from you. That thief could be back here anytime."

"Slow down. Tell me what happened."

"This horrid man brought the kewpie dolls by here about an hour ago. He wants to sell them. I told him I didn't know much about their worth, would have to do some research. I got him to leave the collection with me for a couple of hours."

"Good work, Delbert."

"Yes, yes, but he'll be back soon. I've been worried sick waiting for you to phone. Shouldn't we call the police?"

"Don't do anything yet. I'll come right over."

"But if he comes back—"

"Just stall him. I'll be right there."

"Hurry!"

I hung up the phone, felt for the reassuring lump of my Smith & Wesson at my hip, and hurried back out to the car.

There's no quick way to get to North Fourth Street from where I live, and I cursed and snarled at my fellow motorists as I rushed through traffic.

The gravel parking lot outside Delbert's Dolls was empty when I roared up, but I kept my hand on my pistol as I jingled into the store. Delbert was alone at the counter. Alone except for the hundreds of shiny eyes that stared down from the shelves.

"Oh, thank God it's you, Mr. Mabry."

"Where are the dolls?"

He tilted a cardboard box on the counter so I could see inside. Ten little dolls were lined up in the bottom, smiling up like they were happy to see me. I hadn't brought the Polaroids with me, but there was no question this was Alice Burden's collection. And it looked intact except for one doll on the end, an old number with pink and red feathers. I recognized it as the carny's love gift, and it made me heartsick to see

226

its face had been crushed. Someone had awkwardly tried to arrange the shattered porcelain into some kind of symmetry, but I could tell at a glance it was beyond repair.

"These are the ones, all right."

"Can I call the police now?"

"Sure, go ahead."

Delbert's hand was on the phone when the bell at the door jangled. He turned, froze, squeaked, "That's him."

I wheeled to find Pirate standing in the door, the scarf pulled tight over his head. He wore jeans and motorcycle boots and a tank top to show off his tattooed biceps.

"You?"

"Bubba?"

I fumbled with my holster, pulled my gun and aimed it at him. His eyes went wide for a second, then narrowed, like he was calculating a leap backward through the door.

"Come on in," I said, and my voice hardly shook at all.

Pirate stepped away from the door, closer to me. He scratched at his beard and gave me a practiced prison-yard squint, sizing me up.

"That's close enough." He stopped moving, looked like he was trying not to grin at my nervousness.

"Aw, Pirate, what are you doing stealing dolls?"

I don't know why I bothered. I knew he'd only lie.

"What dolls? Oh, those? Aw, man, my old lady found 'em somewhere. I thought they might be worth something. They hot or something?"

"Don't bullshit me, Pirate."

He fought back a grin. "Couldn't help myself, Bubba. Saw that little house sitting there, and I had to give it a try."

"That house belongs to a city councilwoman."

"Really? She had some nice things. I would've carried off a bunch of stuff, except I was on my bike. Those dolls fit in the saddlebags."

"Well, I hate to do this, Pirate, but we're going to have to call the cops. Go ahead, Delbert."

My back was toward Delbert, but I heard the phone receiver clank onto the floor from his sweaty palms. I yanked my head around, and Pirate saw his opportunity.

A tall shelf of dolls came crashing down on me, knocking the gun from my hand and sending me sprawling in an avalanche of Barbies and Gunds. I landed on my elbow, which oomphed the wind out of me, and rolled over in time to see a steel-toed boot winging toward my head. I threw up a hand, which somehow clutched a teddy bear, and warded off the kick with a snout.

Delbert shrieked like a rabbit in a trap.

The next kick caught me in the shoulder as I scrambled to my feet, slipping and sliding on pandas and pinafores. The kick knocked me over, but I kept my feet under me in a squat. Pirate closed in, and I lunged forward like a linebacker and caught him in the gut with my shoulder.

We crashed to the floor, me on top, and I tried to get my knees on his arms to hold him down. He flung me forward with his knees, past his head, and my chin nearly plowed a furrow in the hardwood floor. Pirate pushed at my legs, trying to get untangled, and I kicked and squirmed and generally did all I could to keep him occupied. If only Delbert would stop screaming and dial 911.

We scrambled to our feet. I glanced around for a weapon, anything that wasn't plush and pretty and Good Housekeeping approved for safety. My gun was somewhere on the floor, but I couldn't see it in the ankle-deep clutter of dolls. I grabbed the other tall shelving unit that stood in the center of the room and tipped it, trying to bury Pirate under a cascade of Muppets and Chatty Cathys.

The shelves caught him on the shoulder and staggered him, but he didn't fall. He pushed at the shelves with an elbow, trying to right them, get them out of the way.

Delbert finally managed to articulate something: "My babies! My beautiful babies!"

"Shut up and call the cops!"

Pirate was on me again, trying to beat me clear of the door. I kept my fists high to protect my face as the heavy blows landed right and left. I threw a couple of my own, even connected to his jaw, but he didn't seem to notice.

I caught his fist with my ear, which made a whine go off inside my head. As I reeled, Pirate pushed past me, headed for the door. I leaped onto his back and hung on for dear life.

I got my left arm around his neck and started hurting my right hand on his skull, popping him again and again, trying to find someplace he'd feel it.

Pirate made a sound like an angry bull and pivoted, trying to swing me off his back. He reached backward with raking hands, but I clung closer and he couldn't get hold of me. He spun around, and the whole world seemed to tilt and buck. Centrifugal force swung my legs out wide and I could feel my feet clearing shelves and smashing dolls.

Glass shattered, and the room was filled with a clanging bell, loud enough to send you running outside if you weren't busy riding a bronco biker.

My shinbones cracked across the edge of a shelf, making me gasp. One of Pirate's grasping fingers stuck me in the eye and I went flying.

I was still between him and the door, holding my eye, and he took a step backward to get a running start to leap over me. Dolls lay everywhere around me. I grabbed one and threw it into Pirate's face.

The flying plaything surprised him. "Hey!"

I grabbed two more, hurled them blindly in his direction. If I could just stall him a little longer . . .

Pirate caught one of the flung dolls and threw it back at me, beaning me upside the head as I clambered to my feet. I grabbed a three-foot-high plastic model by the foot and started swinging it like a saber, thrashing at him. The doll's eyes rolled open and closed and her little dress was up around her waist and Delbert still screamed somewhere as I flailed away.

Pirate lost his footing on the fallen dolls as he backed away, and sat down hard on the floor. I whopped him over the head with the big doll, hard enough that her leg came off in my hand and the rest went flying.

Then, over the deafening alarm and Pirate's curses and Delbert's screams, someone shouted, "Hold it!"

I turned to find two cops crowding through the door, guns drawn.

"Boy," I yelled over the din, "am I glad to see you."

The cops scowled at me, and the nearest one shouted to Delbert, "Turn off that goddamn noise!"

The flushed-faced little man fumbled under the counter, and the clanging died and everybody took a deep breath.

"Now, you," the cop said to me, "drop it."

Drop it? Drop what? I discovered the doll's leg still in my hand. Hardly a deadly weapon, but I did as I was told.

"Now what the hell is going on here?"

It took an hour to get it all explained while Pirate sat locked in a squad car outside. We located my gun under one of the shelves, which helped verify my story. Having the cops recognize me from my picture in the *Gazette* didn't hurt, either.

Delbert was no help, too busy weeping over his shattered inventory, picking up Pooh bears and straightening wedding gowns.

At one point he cried, "You'll pay for all this damage, or I'll sue your pants off!"

The cops turned me loose after I pledged to go Downtown and make a full report. They took the doll collection for evidence, but I persuaded them to let me keep one of the dolls so I could show my client. It would've been natural to select one of the intact dolls, break it to her gently, but I fished the broken one out of the box and carried it carefully out to my car.

My eye was bloodshot and my ear still rang and various aches and bruises made me shuffle along like a bent old man. But I'd won. Pirate was under arrest, the dolls were recovered, and I could, for once, take good news to a client.

I wasn't sure where I'd find Alice Burden on the day of a primary election vote, but I tried her house, and her shiny old Mercedes was out front. I parked the Chevy in the shade of an elm and carried the broken doll to her front door.

Alice was headed out somewhere, all decked out in a navy-blue suit and a wide hat with its brim pinned up flat in the front. Like a cavalry hat, off *F Troop*. She smiled when she saw it was me, but her gaze dropped to the shattered kewpie in my hands and tears sprang to her eyes.

"Oh, I'm sorry," she said, wiping at her eyes. "Foolish old woman. Come in."

I stuttered through assurances that the rest of the dolls were fine, but she took the broken one from me and set it in her lap and stroked its bedraggled feathers.

"How did this one get broken?"

"I don't know. It was that way when I found it. The burglar probably dropped it. He's not the delicate sort."

I gave her a quick account of the doll store fight, making myself sound only a little more valiant than I'd actually been.

"A lot of dolls got busted up in the fight. The guy who owns the place said he'd sue me for the damages. I guess he'll have to, because there's no way I can cover it."

"Don't worry about that," Alice said. "I can take care of it. How much do you think it will be?"

"I don't know. Hundreds of dollars, maybe more. Those dolls aren't cheap."

Alice frowned, like she hadn't expected that much.

"I'll tell you what," she said in a tone that sounded like a council chamber bargain being struck, "I'll talk to the man, see how much he wants, see if I can talk him down. Then I'll match your fee dollar for dollar in paying for the damages. Whatever's left of your fee, I'll send to you."

A little fuzzy math told me that would amount to nothing. No fee from Alice Burden, and nothing from the murder case but the initial retainer from Sultan Sweeney. That and the publicity, which Felicia swore would be good for business. It had better be. The rent was due, and Bongo Patel wasn't a very understanding sort at the first of the month. Not to mention the IRS.

As she walked me to the door, Alice said, "I saw your picture in the paper today. You've been a busy man."

"Yeah, I'm feeling it, too. I need a soak in a hot bath."

She stopped at the door, held out a hand to be shaken.

"Thank you, Bubba. For everything."

"You're welcome. I'm sorry that one doll got broken. I know how much it meant to you."

Her smile faltered, then flickered back to life. Tears shone in her eyes.

"Ah, well, maybe this will finally get that silly old romance out of my system."

24

That night, I tagged along with Felicia to the Dudley victory party. It was the last event in the world Felicia wanted to cover, and she was certain that was why Whitworth assigned it to her. Having me there might keep her from getting into arguments, I told myself, though it had never worked before.

A hot bath and a nap and a couple of drinks had done little to soothe my aching muscles. I'd finally read McMurray's story in the *Gazette,* and that hadn't made me feel any better. Everything had been fine until I neared the end and found a couple of background paragraphs reminding readers about the Elvis business. So much for good publicity.

Felicia, when I met her at the Marriott, still steamed over the story, which she thought made Dudley and Jericho look like heroes. As she'd predicted, Dudley had killed his opponent at the voting booths, and Felicia blamed Whitworth for that, too.

I followed her down a long corridor lined with fake-crystal lamps and large, ornate primping mirrors. We could hear the victory party before we reached the ballroom door.

Inside, it was even louder. Dudley's fundamentalist followers were feeling festive, hooting and hollering and swilling their red Hawaiian Punch. A Dixieland band of old white guys in straw boaters whanged away in one corner. Balloons floated near the ceiling, trailing patriotic streamers. A giant scarlet banner behind the stage said DUDLEY. I worried Felicia might barf.

She scanned the crowd until she found the other reporters, then marched over to them, me following. As we approached, a hair-sprayed guy I recognized from TV snapped to a salute and said, "Hail the conquering heroes of the front page."

"Up yours, Marcus," Felicia growled. She put her hands on her hips and gave the rest of them the hard eye until they looked away, muttering.

A fat guy in a wilted tuxedo approached the podium and called for the crowd's attention, which brought the noise down a few decibels. The guy had the wolfish grin of a car salesman.

"Ladies and gentlemen, it gives me great pleasure to present our re-elected councilman, the Honorable Quentin Dudley."

I'd turned to Felicia, who made a face at the word "honorable." Whatever I'd been going to say slipped my mind.

Dudley strode through a door behind the low stage and waved his arms above his head as his supporters cheered and whistled. Marilyn Dudley and Jericho followed, the reverend grasping Marilyn's elbow to help her up the two steps onto the dais.

The fat guy stepped aside, jiggling as he hammered his palms together, grinning like a pike. Dudley couldn't resist the urge to tap the microphone with his hand to make sure it was working before he began the customary victory gloat. Television lights flicked on all around me, washing out colors with their glare.

Dudley thanked his supporters for their hard work.

He thanked Marilyn for her sacrifices, but she just stared glassily at the crowd. He thanked Jericho, who waved and tipped his head solemnly to the applause.

"The hard work isn't over yet," Dudley said, and that sobered the crowd a little. "I heard today the Democrats are scrambling around, looking for a write-in candidate to run against us in November."

Felicia looked up from her notebook, saw me watching her, shrugged. A write-in campaign was news to her, too.

Dudley didn't mention that his Democratic opponent had dropped dead, but a certain smugness swept through the room, as if the supporters knew it was God's will that no one stand in Quentin Dudley's way.

"Beyond that," he continued, "there's still the work we have to do on Central Avenue. Despite what our friends in the media might think—" He gestured to the clump of reporters, who shuffled uncomfortably at the attention. "—cleaning up Central wasn't just some campaign ploy. It's a job we intend to finish."

The audience clapped wildly, ready to saddle up and resume their Holy Crusade. The whole thing made me queasy.

After another round of thanks, Dudley stepped back from the microphone, raised his hands, and clenched them over his head in the classic victory pose. Cameras flashed, the crowd roared, the band struck up a caterwaul, and Dudley took his time leaving the stage. Marilyn and Jericho followed him.

Their departure—back to their suite to savor more election returns, no doubt—left a hole in the celebration, one that would be filled with drinking at the typical political function. No alcohol was available— I'd already checked—but these folks glowed with victory and virtue. They didn't look like they'd be running home soon to liberate their babysitters. They were having too much good, clean fun.

The reporters were another matter. The TV cameras turned on the talking-head types to do live feeds, and the rest of the pack hurried out to file their stories, looking relieved to escape so much jubilation. Felicia tugged at my sleeve.

"Let's go. I've got to call the office."

I nodded and followed her through the crowd, nearly walked up her back when she stopped suddenly near the door.

"I'll be damned," she muttered, drawing looks from some of the nearby believers. "Look over there, Bubba. Is that who I think it is?"

I followed her eyes, but saw nobody I recognized. Just more cheering Dudleyites. Beyond them, though, hanging near the wall, was a woman in big sunglasses and a head scarf, which seemed odd attire for indoors, at night.

"Who?"

"Don't you know who that is?"

"The woman in the sunglasses?"

"Yes. You don't recognize her? It's Rosie Corona. Now what do you suppose she's doing here?"

Felicia made her way through the crowd to Rosie. I hung back, not wanting another tangle with the SCORE organizer.

Rosie tried to turn away as Felicia approached, but we had her cornered, and she crossed her arms defensively and awaited Felicia's questions.

"You're about the last person I'd expect to see at Dudley's party," Felicia said.

Rosie looked from Felicia to me and back again.

"Well, I wouldn't expect to see you with someone like *him.*"

Felicia shrugged it off, moved closer to Rosie so they could talk quietly. I strained to hear over the crowd noise.

"So what are you doing here?" Felicia asked her.

"I was just wondering that myself." Bitterness in her voice.

"What do you mean?"

"I mean, I just can't believe myself sometimes. After all Quentin Dudley has done and all he's said about prostitutes, here I am, waiting for him."

"Waiting for him?"

Rosie looked away, thinking over how much she should say. When she turned back to Felicia, her lips were set tight.

"Yeah, waiting for him. Quentin always likes a tumble after he wins an election."

I about fell off my shoes at this news, but Felicia just nodded, scratched something in her notebook.

"But why you? Why doesn't he chase his wife around if he's feeling randy?"

"Have you seen his wife?"

"Yeah, I've met her."

"Would you want to sleep with that cold fish?"

"Well, no . . ."

Rosie looked impatient.

"Look, Quentin Dudley's been a client of mine for years. I never minded keeping it discreet, but since he's started this crusade, I think we're working opposite sides of the street."

The demonstration flashed into my mind, the way Rosie's girls had hissed "hypocrite" at every mention of Dudley's name.

Rosie Corona shook her head, looked down at her fingernails. "Maybe I'll just leave. I don't know why I came here at all. I can't imagine letting that man touch me again."

She edged along the wall, but Felicia stepped sideways and cut her off.

"Wait a minute. Can you prove you've had this relationship with him? Something you know, maybe nobody else knows?"

Rosie thought it over for a second, then a trace of a smile surfaced on her face.

"Well, there is that brown mole on his cock. He calls it his beauty mark. I imagine not many have seen that."

Felicia rose up on her toes, but her voice was calm as she said, "Come on, there's someone I want you to meet."

She took Rosie's arm and led her toward the corridor. I tried to follow, but Felicia said, "You wait here."

I drifted around the edges of the crowd, thought about sneaking off to Nicole's, the bar off the Marriott lobby, decided against it. I didn't know what Felicia was up to, but I didn't want to miss anything.

Reverend Skip Jericho reappeared on the stage, tapped the mike, boomed into it, "Good evening, brothers and sisters!"

The crowd cheered and clustered closer to the stage, eager for the words of their revered oracle.

"Councilman Dudley asked me to come out here and speak to you all, express again how grateful he is for all your help."

Jericho waited for the applause to subside, then said, "And I reminded him it was high time we gave thanks to the One who makes it all possible. Let us pray."

Heads bowed throughout the ballroom, like everyone there wanted a whack across the neck. I kept my eyes open.

"Dear Father," Jericho began, loud enough so that God wouldn't have any trouble hearing, "we come before you tonight grateful and suppliant, knowing that we're not worthy of all you do for us."

Felicia appeared at my side, out of breath.

"Where have you been?" I whispered.

"Just watch. You'll see."

The door behind the stage opened and Marilyn Dudley stepped through. Her face was bright red and her white-knuckled hands clutched her big handbag in front of her like a shield. She froze when she saw people praying, but didn't bow her head, just stood there glaring at Jericho, twitching and chewing her lower lip.

"We want to thank you, Lord, for helping your servant, Quentin Dudley, prevail in today's election. And we ask for your continued help in our work to make Albuquerque a Christian city, a law-abiding haven of God."

Jericho peeked out from under his brows, saw Marilyn waiting, wrapped it up with an "Amen" that was echoed around the room. I glanced over at Felicia, but she revealed nothing, just beamed at what was to come.

Marilyn strode to the podium. Jericho saw her coming, tried to make it smooth: "And here is the woman behind the successful man—"

"I'll take the microphone now, Reverend," Marilyn said through a clenched jaw.

Jericho scowled, realizing something was wrong. "Just a second, Sister Dudley—"

"Move it, Skip."

Jericho stepped aside, sort of bowed to the seething hostility before him.

Marilyn Dudley cleared her throat, glanced around the room, looked like she was getting cold feet. Then she leaned stiffly forward to speak into the microphone.

"You all know me, and you know I never lie. I learned tonight that my husband, your beloved councilman, is a whoremonger, and that he'll burn in Hell."

A gasp rippled through the crowd. Jericho looked as

if he'd jump straight out of his socks. He reached out toward the microphone, but Marilyn swatted his hand away with her purse.

Quentin Dudley flung open the door behind the stage, looked around hurriedly, like he didn't really expect to find his wife in the ballroom. When he saw her, the color drained from his face. His appearance was met by an awkward silence. Marilyn didn't seem to notice, just kept spitting her invective.

"Quentin's been carrying on for years with a prostitute here in town. That one who's in the newspapers all the time, Rosie Corona. I just received absolute proof from her own lips."

Dudley, looking shaken, hurried across the stage to her, swimming through the silence.

"Do you hear that?" Felicia whispered to me.

"What?"

"That flushing sound. That's Dudley's political future going down the toilet."

Quentin snaked an arm around Marilyn's waist, smiled nervously at the crowd. She tried to push away from him, but he clutched her tightly, began backing her away from the microphone.

"Sinner!" she screamed as she struggled against him. "Whoremonger!"

Jericho snatched the microphone from its stand and tried to explain it away.

"It's clear Sister Dudley isn't feeling well tonight, that she's, um, upset about some, uh, misunderstanding."

The crowd wasn't buying it. People stood frozen in place by the betrayal of their beliefs, watching their hero wrestle his howling wife through the backstage door.

"Let's raise our voices in glory to the Lord!"

Jericho tried "Bringing in the Sheaves" at top

volume, but after a verse, he blushed at the realization he was singing a solo. People began moving grumblingly toward the door.

A shout went up in the corridor and reverberated through the room.

Felicia said, "Uh-oh," and raced away toward the door, elbowing people out of her way. I followed as best I could, though I didn't know what had gone wrong.

A clump of baying churchmen had Rosie Corona treed in the corridor, her back against a wall as they menaced her with words and cold stares. Rosie still wore her sunglasses, and her head was bowed. TV cameras threw white light over the scene, their glare the only thing keeping the angry followers from ripping the Jezebel apart and feeding her to the dogs.

Felicia pushed her way through them, clutched Rosie's arm.

"Back off, you jerks!" she shouted. "All this woman did was tell the truth."

"Harlot!" someone shouted from the back.

I pushed through the last layer of Bible-thumpers and stepped between them and the women. A red-faced man reached out to push me in the chest, but I raised a finger to get his attention and it pulled him up short. I reached behind me, under my shirt, and pulled the snub-nosed Smith & Wesson from its holster. His hand retreated like I'd scalded it.

"The lady said back off. Now do it."

It's easy to sound like Gary Cooper when you're the one holding the gun.

The crowd parted as we edged toward the outside door, and I was able to put the gun away after we rounded a corner. No one dared follow us, crazy sinners that we were.

The night air was cool as we hustled Rosie to her

car. I kept glancing over my shoulder, but none of Jericho's people followed. Even the TV cameramen had held back after seeing the pistol. I could just imagine what the live reports must be saying.

Felicia touched Rosie's shoulder, made her turn before she could duck into her little Honda Civic.

"Thanks," Felicia said. "I didn't mean for you to get caught in there like that and have to take that abuse."

Rosie took off the dark glasses, looked Felicia over.

"I guess I should've left after I talked to that woman, just like you said, but I had to stick around and see what happened."

Felicia nodded understandingly. "So what happens now?" she asked.

"What do you mean?"

"With SCORE. With you."

Rosie's face cracked into a grin, and she glanced around the parking lot before answering.

"You know, I was thinking about that before those guys spotted me. I've been working my ass off, organizing and lobbying, and look how little good it's done. After what happened tonight, I'll be remembered as the hooker who ruined Quentin Dudley's career, not for everything else I've done."

Felicia tried to interrupt, "No, Rosie, you'll—"

Rosie held up a hand and smiled, showing she didn't need to hear it.

"It's okay. But I was thinking, maybe it's time to take advantage of the limelight."

"What do you mean?"

"The Democrats are still going to need somebody to beat Quentin in November. Maybe I'll start a write-in campaign."

Felicia and I looked at each other and laughed, a

high-pitched crazy laugh, anticipating what was to come. Rosie joined in, making a joyful noise over the trouble she'd be starting.

"Politics is just people screwing each other, right?" she said. "I'm an expert."